The Touch of Telly D. Young

Book One of the Telly D. Young Series

James R. Baldwin

"Some gifts are meant to be hidden. Others demand to be seen."

James R. Baldwin

Dedicated to

John Wesley Parker

12.08.1969 - 05.13.2025

John was one of the best people you will ever meet. He passed away during the writing of this book, and he will always and forever be missed.

The Touch of Telly D. Young

Book One of the Telly D. Young Series

© 2025 James R. Baldwin

All rights reserved.

No part of this book may be reproduced, stored in a retrieval system, or transmitted in any form or by any means—electronic, mechanical, photocopying, recording, or otherwise—without the prior written permission of the author, except by a reviewer who may quote brief passages in a review.

This is a work of fiction. Names, characters, places, and incidents either are the product of the author's imagination or are used fictitiously. Any resemblance to actual persons, living or dead, events, or locales is purely coincidental.

Cover Design: James R. Baldwin

Interior Layout: Stacie D. Baldwin

First Edition

ISBN: 9798284853580

Printed in the United States of America

Contents

The Touch of Telly D. Young 1

ONE 12
    The Boy Who Never Cried 12
TWO 16
    The Backyard Miracles 16
THREE 21
    The First Sign 21
FOUR 27
    The Promise 27
FIVE 32
    Tethered 32
SIX 36
    An Urge Too Strong 36
SEVEN 40
    The Argument 40
EIGHT 44
    Training Days 44
NINE 48
    The Secret Shared 48
TEN 51
    A Shift in the Wind 51
ELEVEN 54
    Into the Fold 54
TWELVE 58

The Spark of Suspicion	58
THIRTEEN	62
The Pull	62
FOURTEEN	65
The Rumor Mill	65
FIFTEEN	68
Held Back	68
SIXTEEN	72
The Woman in the Church	72
SEVENTEEN	75
Grace	75
EIGHTEEN	80
The Choice	80
NINETEEN	85
Breaking Point	85
TWENTY	88
Echoes	88
TWENTY-ONE	93
The Visitors	93
TWENTY-TWO	96
The Letter	96
TWENTY-THREE	99
The Town Listens	99
TWENTY-FOUR	103
The Stillness Before	103
TWENTY-FIVE	107

The Breaking News 107
TWENTY-SIX 110
   The Watchers 110
TWENTY-SEVEN 115
   The Line 115
TWENTY-EIGHT 119
   The Choice Repeated 119
TWENTY-NINE 122
   The New Name 122
Part TWO 128
   The Awakened 128
THIRTY 129
   Signals 129
THIRTY-ONE 132
   Coordinates 132
THIRTY-TWO 135
   The Awakened 135
THIRTY-THREE 137
   Names in the Circle 137
THIRTY-FOUR 142
   Contact 142
THIRTY-FIVE 145
   Gathering Light 145
THIRTY-SIX 150
   The Interrogator 150
THIRTY-SEVEN 153

- The Circle Fractures 153
- THIRTY-EIGHT 156
  - Ash 156
- THIRTY-NINE 158
  - Visions in the Fire 158
- FORTY 162
  - The Next Name 162
- FORTY-ONE 164
  - The Raid 164
- FORTY-TWO 167
  - Sacrifice 167
- FORTY-THREE 169
  - Reckoning 169
- FORTY-FOUR 172
  - Ashes and Echoes 172
- FORTY-FIVE 175
  - Blueprints 175
- FORTY-SIX 179
  - The First Beacon 179
- FORTY-SEVEN 182
  - Ripples 182
- FORTY-EIGHT 185
  - Rowan 185
- FORTY-NINE 187
  - Static 187
- FIFTY 191

Echoes in Missouri 191
FIFTY-ONE 194
    Shadows at the Door 194
FIFTY-TWO 197
    Threshold 197
FIFTY-THREE 200
    Crossing Lines 200
FIFTY-FOUR 203
    The Trap 203
FIFTY-FIVE 206
    Confrontation 206
FIFTY-SIX 209
    Fallout 209
FIFTY-SEVEN 211
    The Scars We Carry 211
FIFTY-EIGHT 214
    No More Ghosts 214
FIFTY-NINE 216
    The Signal Breaks 216
SIXTY 219
    Ash Returns 219
SIXTY-ONE 221
    The Uprising 221
SIXTY-TWO 224
    Revelation 224
SIXTY-THREE 227

- The Light We Carry 227
- SIXTY-FOUR 229
  - Last Move 229
- SIXTY-FIVE 232
  - Awakened 232
- Book Two 234
- ONE 235
  - Beneath the Mask 235

James R. Baldwin

Part ONE

ONE

The Boy Who Never Cried
Blue Ridge Mountains
January 1st, 1980

The winter storm swept through the town of Alder Bend, icing tree limbs and blanketing the roads in a thick coat of white. Inside a modest hospital tucked on the edge of the woods, Marianne Young gripped her husband's hand and gave one last push. The room went quiet.

Then—silence. Not the expected wail of a newborn, but a soft hum from the nearby heater and the rustle of snowflakes outside the window. The baby blinked.

His eyes were open wide, crystal blue, and focused. The nurse gasped.

"He's... not crying," she whispered.

Dr. Ramirez bent close, checked his vitals, and smiled despite the oddity. "He's perfectly healthy."

James Young stepped forward, placing his palm on his son's chest. "Telly," he said quietly, a name they'd agreed on months ago. "Telly D. Young."

The boy gripped his father's finger and smiled.

By the time he was five, Telly had never had so much as a cold. No fevers, no cuts that lasted more than a few minutes. One afternoon, while exploring the pine woods near their home, he slipped and sliced his palm on a broken branch. Blood dripped briefly. Then stopped. The wound closed before his eyes.

He ran home, showing Marianne the faint line on his hand.

She stared at it for a long time. "Did you put something on it?"

Telly shook his head.

James came in from chopping wood. Marianne showed him the mark, now barely visible. They exchanged a long glance.

Later that night, after Telly was asleep, they spoke in hushed voices in the kitchen.

"He's never been sick," Marianne said. "Not once. No fever, no cough, not even a scraped knee that lasted more than an hour."

James nodded. "I've been thinking the same. But that hand—Marianne, it looked like it sealed itself."

She looked worried. "We can't jump to conclusions. But... we need to watch him more closely. Just in case."

James said nothing, but inside, a slow unease began to take root.

One evening, as snow fell outside their cabin, the family gathered for evening prayer. Telly, restless and innocent, knelt between his parents. James rested his hand on his son's shoulder, a gentle but firm weight.

Outside, through the frost-laced window, a fox limped past—a fresh gash on its leg. It stopped, shuddered, and then... straightened. With a slow stride, it walked calmly into the woods, the wound gone.

Inside, the flames flickered in the hearth as James looked into the fire. He knew.

James R. Baldwin

TWO

The Backyard Miracles
Blue Ridge Mountains
1987

Telly was seven when he started noticing strange things happening around the cabin—things he never told his parents.

It began with a bird.

A blue jay had slammed into the kitchen window one morning while Telly was helping Marianne water the houseplants. The sharp thud made them both jump. Marianne gasped and ran out to check.

"It's dead," she said with a sigh, gently picking up the tiny body and placing it on the porch rail.

But after she went back inside to get a towel, Telly stepped closer. The bird's eye was open, glassy, and still. He reached out, touched its wing.

In a blink, the bird fluttered, stumbled upright, and flew off in a blue blur.

Telly stood frozen.

He said nothing. Not even when his mom came back, confused to find the rail empty.

A few days later, Telly was in the backyard when he heard a loud thump and a squeal from behind the woodshed. James had just mowed a narrow path through the tall grass near the edge of the property. Telly ran toward the sound and found a small rabbit writhing in the grass, its side bloodied and one ear mangled.

His father didn't see it—he had already turned the mower off and was coiling the extension cord, humming to himself. Telly knelt beside the rabbit, his chest tight.

He looked at its shallow breathing, its trembling legs. The pain was real, the fear in its eyes deeper than anything he'd ever seen. Instinctively, he reached out and laid his hand on the rabbit's side.

A soft warmth pulsed from his fingers. The bleeding stopped. The twitching slowed.

Moments later, the rabbit jerked once, then righted itself. It hesitated, nose twitching, then bounded off into the woods—its gait steady, the wound completely vanished.

Telly sat back, breathless. That hadn't been an accident. That had been something else.

Something only he could do.

Telly just stared at his hand.

It kept happening.

A barn cat caught a chipmunk and left it in the grass, unmoving. Telly picked it up gently, whispering an apology.

Moments later, it wriggled free and darted away.

He began wondering if he was doing something wrong—if he was breaking nature's rules. Shouldn't the dead stay dead? Were these animals really okay, or was he just imagining things?

He tried to talk to Pastor Eli about it once, vaguely. He asked if animals went to heaven, and if God ever sent them back.

Eli had smiled, tousled his hair, and said, "Sometimes I think animals understand God better than we do."

That didn't answer his question.

One evening, Telly sat on the porch steps, arms on his knees, watching the sky darken. The woods glowed gold in the last light. He had just helped a sparrow that had fallen from the chicken coop roof.

He didn't feel scared, exactly. But he didn't feel normal either.

He hadn't been sick a day in his life. He couldn't remember ever needing a bandage for more than a few minutes.

Now, animals were getting back up after he touched them.

Something wasn't right.

But he didn't tell his parents.

Not yet.

He wasn't sure how.

THREE

The First Sign
Blue Ridge Mountains, 1988

The morning air was crisp, and a thin veil of fog rolled over the ground as James and eight-year-old Telly walked side by side through the woods behind their mountain property. It was the last day of pheasant season—mid-December—and the cold bit deeper than usual, adding urgency to their steps. The forest was thick with pine, spruce, and naked-limbed maples, stretching for miles across the ridgelines of northern Georgia. Their cabin sat tucked at the base of a hill, about thirty yards from a slow-running creek. A narrow deer trail led directly from their backyard into the heart of the woods—a route James had followed since he was a boy himself.

Telly wore his oversized camouflage jacket, sleeves bundled at the wrists, and boots that crunched softly over damp leaves. The sky was pale with the promise of dawn, and the forest stirred with hidden life—woodpeckers drumming, a distant rustle of deer. His cheeks stung from the cold, but he never complained. These hunting mornings with his father felt like sacred time.

James adjusted the shotgun over his shoulder and glanced down at his son. "Quiet steps, buddy. The birds won't wait for us to talk about it."

They moved deeper into the woods, following the old loggers' path to a clearing ringed with brush—an ideal pheasant spot James had used for years. Here, the trees opened up to a flat stretch of frosty ground, where the mist hovered low. A few rocks marked the edges, and an old tree stump still bore the rusted tin can targets James had nailed there for practice.

James raised the shotgun. A pheasant, startled from the brush, took flight.

Crack!

The shot rang out and echoed. The bird dropped into the underbrush.

James motioned to Telly. "Go fetch it."

Telly jogged over, brushing aside brittle leaves and twigs. The bird lay still—its feathers ruffled, wing bent awkwardly. He knelt, hesitating. Something stirred in his chest. Not pity, exactly. Something deeper.

He reached out, both hands trembling slightly, and lifted the bird.

Its chest rose. Then again. The wing shifted, then snapped back into place with a soft pop. Telly's eyes widened.

The pheasant blinked, flapped once, and took off—right from his hands.

Behind him, branches cracked under his father's boots. "Telly?"

He turned slowly.

James stared—not at Telly, but at the empty spot where the bird had fallen. "Where's the pheasant?"

"I... I picked it up. It was hurt, but... it flew away."

James's face went pale. His voice dropped. "Did you touch it?"

Telly nodded.

Without another word, James took his hand and led him back down the trail.

Their home sat low to the ground, a two-bedroom log cabin built by James's father. A stone chimney jutted out the back, sending up a thin ribbon of smoke. Inside, the walls were lined with pine paneling, and the air always smelled of cedar and coffee. The living room and kitchen shared one large space, with a long wooden table near the window and a worn leather couch facing the fireplace. One narrow hallway led to the bedrooms and a single bathroom.

Marianne stood at the stove, wearing her usual morning robe and house shoes. She turned as they entered, concern flashing in her eyes.

"What happened?"

James didn't speak until Telly was sent to his room.

Marianne watched him closely as he pulled off his boots and sank into the chair by the fireplace. The fire crackled quietly between them.

"It happened," James said finally, his voice low. "The bird came back. He touched it, and it... flew off like nothing happened."

Marianne froze, spatula in hand, eggs forgotten on the stove.

"Are you sure?"

"I saw the spot it dropped. There was no other bird. And he told me—he picked it up. The wing was busted, Marianne. And then it flew."

She sat down across from him slowly, placing both hands in her lap.

"We've been praying this wouldn't happen. We knew it was possible, but... he's still a boy. He doesn't understand."

James stared at the flames. "It's more than that. He didn't just touch it. "He healed it," James said quietly. "Like the hand of God reached through him."

Marianne shook her head, her eyes full of worry. "James, they won't see it that way. People won't call it a miracle—they'll tear it apart. They'll come for him. We can't let that happen."

"I know," James replied, his jaw tightening. "This stays with us. We teach him to stay quiet. No more hunting. No more risks."

Marianne's voice broke. "He's just a child, James. He needs school, friends—some chance at a normal life."

James looked at her, eyes filled with a kind of exhausted sadness. "He's not normal, Marianne. And God help us—we've got to protect him like he's the last piece of something holy."

From behind the thin wall, Telly heard the hush of their voices. He didn't understand the words exactly, but he understood their weight—heavy, secret, dangerous.

His mother's whisper broke the silence one last time.

"We can't let the world find out."

Telly lay in bed, curled beneath the covers. His room was small, just big enough for a bed, a tall dresser, and a shelf lined with books and plastic army men. He stared at the ceiling. He didn't understand what he had done. But somehow, it had made his parents afraid.

And that fear found its way into his heart too.

The next morning, the woods seemed farther away than ever before.

FOUR

The Promise
Blue Ridge Mountains
1989

The next morning, the house felt different—like something had shifted just slightly out of place. Telly sat at the breakfast table, his cereal going soggy in the bowl. He absently stirred it with his spoon, round and round, never lifting it to his mouth. James sat at the far end of the table with his coffee, staring into the dark liquid like it held answers. Marianne moved through the kitchen distractedly, touching the toaster, opening a drawer, and wiping the already-clean counter.

The air inside the house felt warm from the woodstove, but there was a stillness beneath the comfort, a tension like frost clinging to the windows that refused to melt.

Finally, James set his mug down with a quiet thunk. "Telly," he said, gently but firmly, "come sit with us in the living room for a minute."

Telly followed, feet padding over the worn rug as he settled into the cushions of the couch. The fire crackled nearby, casting shifting light across the room. His parents sat across from him in the two soft chairs that flanked the hearth—faces serious but kind.

James leaned forward, elbows on his knees. "Son, what you did yesterday... with the bird... that's not something everyone can do."

Telly didn't respond. He stared down at his hands resting in his lap, the same hands that had cupped the wounded pheasant just hours ago, and watched it come back to life.

Marianne reached out and gently touched his shoulder. Her fingers were soft and trembling. "We think... we believe God has given you a gift."

Telly looked up, his eyes wide. "Is it bad?" he asked, his voice small.

"No," she said quickly, her voice catching slightly. "It's not bad. But it's... it's something the world might not understand. And some people, Telly... they don't always treat special things kindly."

James nodded slowly. "That's why we need to ask you something important. Can you keep this to yourself? Just for now?"

Telly furrowed his brow. "Like a secret?"

"Yes," James said, his voice quiet but firm. "Not because we're ashamed. But because this world can be cruel. And people might try to use you, or hurt you, or take you away from us."

A long moment passed. Telly swallowed hard, the weight of the request sinking in.

Then he nodded. "Okay," he whispered. "I promise."

Marianne leaned over and pulled him close, wrapping her arms around him like she could protect him from everything outside their walls. The fire popped in the hearth, and the wind outside moaned faintly through the trees.

That Sunday, they went to church.

The sky was gray and heavy with the weight of late winter. Snow still clung in patches beneath the trees, but the roads were mostly clear. The little chapel sat at the end of the gravel lane, nestled against a stand of evergreens that whispered in the wind.

Inside, it was warm and hushed. The wooden pews creaked under familiar weight. Candles flickered. Pastor Eli stood at the front, his voice rich and smooth as he preached about unseen blessings and quiet miracles.

Telly sat between his parents, hands folded tightly in his lap. He stared at the stained-glass windows—blue, red, and gold light bending across the floor—and wondered if any of those saints had ever been asked to hide.

After the service, while adults murmured their goodbyes and children pulled at coats and mittens, Pastor Eli approached him near the pews.

"How are you holding up, Telly?" he asked, crouching to meet the boy's eyes.

Telly looked down. "Okay."

Eli offered a quiet smile. "You know," he said, "sometimes God gives certain people a secret gift. But it's not always easy knowing what to do with it."

Telly hesitated. "How do you know what to do?"

The pastor placed a warm hand on his shoulder. "You listen. To your heart, to your family... and to God. He'll show you."

That evening, as the last sliver of sunlight bled behind the hills, Telly stepped outside alone.

The woods behind the house were still, cloaked in frost. The clearing where it had all happened was quiet now, the earth firm and dark. He walked slowly, boots crunching on the brittle grass, breath puffing pale into the cold air.

He knelt down where the bird had lain, pressed his fingers to the dirt. It was damp. Cold. Alive.

"I won't let anyone find out," he whispered.

The forest gave no reply. No wind. No birdcall.

But something in his chest settled with the words—like a vow, spoken aloud and etched into the bones of the trees around him. He hadn't just made a promise to his parents.

He had made it to himself.

FIVE

Tethered

Blue Ridge Mountains

1990

Winter deepened. Snow piled higher along the porch rails. Telly stayed close to home, the cabin warm but quieter now. James no longer suggested morning hikes. Marianne's voice was gentler, her prayers longer.

Though nothing had been said since that morning, the air around his gift hung like smoke—seen but never spoken of.

One gray afternoon, Telly stood by the window, watching a deer graze near the treeline. A buck with a bent leg limped into view, then lowered itself into the snow.

He pressed his hand to the glass. A part of him wanted to run outside and help. Another part reminded him of the promise.

He turned away.

At night, his dreams changed. He saw flashes of light, heard the cries of animals he'd healed, watched himself walk through rooms full of strangers who reached for him with desperate eyes. Sometimes he woke in a cold sweat. Other times with tears.

One morning at breakfast, James noticed.

"You sleep okay, bud?"

Telly shrugged. "I dream too much."

Marianne looked over, hesitating. "Sometimes dreams are how God helps us practice. For when we're awake."

Telly nodded, unsure if that helped.

Later that week, Pastor Eli came by to deliver firewood. He brought cinnamon rolls from his wife and stayed for tea.

When James stepped out to the shed, Eli turned to Telly.

"You still thinking about our talk?"

Telly nodded. "I think about it a lot."

Pastor Eli leaned forward. "God doesn't always give answers right away. But when He does, it's not with a loud voice. It's with peace."

Telly whispered, "It doesn't feel peaceful."

Eli smiled gently. "That's how you know it's not time yet."

That night, Telly stood by the hearth while his parents read quietly nearby. He reached out his hand toward the flames—not close enough to touch, just far enough to feel the heat on his palm.

He wondered if the warmth he felt when healing was like this—part fire, part faith.

He pulled his hand back and sat cross-legged on the rug, staring into the blaze.

He would wait.

But deep down, the pull was getting harder to ignore.

James R. Baldwin

SIX

An Urge Too Strong
Blue Ridge Mountains
1991

It was late February when the silence finally broke. Snowmelt ran in slow streams down the hillside, revealing patches of muddy earth and tired, brown grass that wound like old trails around the cabin. The chill still clung to the air, but the forest was stirring—birds beginning to return, branches shifting with the early signs of spring.

Telly was ten now. Taller, quieter, with a habit of drifting into thought and staying there for hours. He spent long afternoons reading by the window, sketching trees in a notebook, or walking alone just far enough that he could still see the house.

But the pull—the inner voice, the heat in his palms—was louder.

The day it happened, Marianne was in town for supplies. James was chopping wood. Telly had wandered behind the chicken coop when he heard the sound: a low, whimpering cry from under the porch.

He crouched down and peered into the dark crawlspace. A small beagle puppy—no more than a few months old—lay trembling in the shadows, its leg bent at an unnatural angle. Mud and dried blood covered its side. It had probably been hit by a passing car on the nearby dirt road.

Telly called softly. "Hey, it's okay. Come here."

The puppy whimpered again. Telly lay on his stomach and crawled halfway under the porch, arms outstretched. He reached the pup and gently pulled it toward him.

The moment he touched it, his hands lit with warmth.

He didn't hesitate.

His fingers moved over the dog's leg, his breathing slow, eyes half-closed. The warmth spread—through his chest, into his arms, through his hands. The leg shifted. The whimpering stopped.

A moment later, the dog stood, shook itself off, and licked his face.

Telly laughed—a sharp, breathless sound. He wrapped his arms around the puppy and whispered, "You're okay. You're okay now."

When James found him half an hour later, sitting on the back porch with the puppy curled in his lap, he froze.

"What is that?" he asked.

Telly looked up. "He was hurt. I think a car hit him. But he's okay now."

James didn't move. His eyes flicked from the dog to Telly's hands.

"You didn't tell me first," he said softly.

"I couldn't wait," Telly said. "He was hurting."

James let out a slow breath. He didn't scold. He just sat beside his son and scratched the pup behind the ears.

After a while, he said, "We're going to have to talk about this again. Soon."

Telly nodded. "I know."

He looked down at the puppy in his lap.

The gift was growing.

And it was getting harder to ignore.

James R. Baldwin

SEVEN

The Argument
Blue Ridge Mountains
1992

That evening, after dinner dishes were washed and the wood stove crackled softly in the living room, Telly fell asleep with the puppy curled up tight against his feet. The little creature let out a quiet sigh in its dreams, warm and safe for the first time in days.

Down the hall, the rest of the house fell into hush.

In the kitchen, the lights were dim. The only sound came from the old refrigerator, humming in a steady rhythm that sounded almost like breathing.

James sat at the kitchen table, elbows on the worn wood, fingers laced, jaw clenched so tightly it looked like he was grinding his thoughts into stone. A coffee mug sat untouched beside him—cold and half full.

Marianne stood by the sink, her back to him at first. Arms crossed. Shoulders stiff.

"He didn't even hesitate," James finally said, his voice low and tight. "Didn't look around. Didn't think twice."

Marianne turned halfway toward him, eyes steady but not angry. "He's a child," she said. "He saw something suffering and he acted. What else did you expect him to do?"

James stared toward the hallway where the boy slept. "I expected him to remember the promise."

The word hung heavy in the air.

Marianne stepped away from the sink. Her expression softened, but her voice didn't lose its edge. "So did I. But it's not fair to ask a ten-year-old to carry that kind of weight forever. Especially not when he sees what he can do. Who he can help."

James shook his head. "He healed a dog in broad daylight, Mari. On the side of the road. That pup was dead, and now it's chasing rabbits through our yard. You think people won't notice? What happens when the neighbors start asking where it came from? When someone puts the pieces together?"

She turned fully now, crossing the room with slow, deliberate steps. "And what happens if he starts believing that his gift is something to be afraid of? Something shameful?"

Her voice caught a little. "What happens if we make him hide it for so long that he forgets how to use it at all?"

James didn't answer. He looked down at his hands—so used to building, to holding, to protecting—and felt how useless they were against this kind of fear. Against what they couldn't see coming.

Marianne sat across from him. "I'm scared too. Every day. But fear can't be the only voice he hears. We've done our best to protect him, James. Maybe it's time we start preparing him instead."

James exhaled slowly, the lines in his face deeper than usual. His voice cracked when he finally spoke. "Then we have to be smart. No more hiding without purpose. We teach him how to be careful. How to choose the right moments. Not just follow rules... but follow wisdom."

She reached across the table and placed her hand over his, steady and warm.

"Then let's start tomorrow," she said.

James nodded. Not as a father with all the answers—but as one willing to try again.

Outside, the wind picked up, brushing against the windows with the sound of change.

And down the hall, the boy slept on, unaware of the weight being lifted from his shoulders—just a little.

Enough for now.

James R. Baldwin

EIGHT

Training Days
Blue Ridge Mountains
1993

James started small. They walked the woods together again—just the two of them. Not for hunting this time, but for quiet talks and watchful learning. The woods were still deep with snowmelt in places, the scent of wet pine and thawing earth filling the air.

James taught Telly how to move softly through the trees, how to look instead of stare. He showed him how to read the forest like a story: broken branches, crushed grass, paw prints pressed into mud. Every mark meant something.

"You have to see things before others do," James said one morning as they knelt beside a set of fresh deer tracks. "That's how you stay ahead. That's how you stay safe."

Telly nodded, eyes sharp, his breath misting in the cold air. He listened carefully—more carefully than most boys his age ever would.

At home, Marianne helped in her own quiet way.

Each morning after breakfast, she had Telly read a few verses from Proverbs aloud. She didn't rush him. They paused often to talk about what the words meant. Wisdom. Restraint. Trust.

"People with gifts often walk alone," she said one day, folding laundry as Telly read. "But that doesn't mean they walk without purpose."

She shared stories, too—biblical, fictional, historical, about heroes and prophets, loners, and leaders. She wanted him to know he wasn't the first to carry something bigger than himself.

They gave him more to do around the house. Feeding the chickens. Stacking firewood. Leading the dinner prayer. Little things, but they mattered. They taught him rhythm. Routine. Purpose.

And always—gently—they encouraged him to keep the puppy close. Not hidden. Not flaunted. Just there. Just his.

A boy and his dog.

Some nights, when the house had gone quiet and the world outside was dark, Telly would sneak downstairs and sit by the fireplace with the pup curled at his side.

While it slept, he'd place his hands just above its back and close his eyes.

He wasn't trying to heal. He wasn't trying to change anything. He was trying to feel.

There was something like a hum—an invisible thread between him and the creature. Sometimes it pulsed like a heartbeat. Other times it was still.

But more and more, he could call it. Not always. But often. And when it came, he wasn't afraid anymore.

He had stopped wondering what he was.

Now he was starting to ask why.

And what he might become.

James R. Baldwin

NINE

The Secret Shared
Blue Ridge Mountains
1994

Spring came early that year. The snow melted quickly into swollen creeks, and green shoots pushed up through soft patches of earth. Telly and Derrick Holloway, his best and only friend, met often in the clearing by the creek where their fathers used to fish together. It was one of the few places their parents trusted them to wander alone.

Derrick was a year older and bolder in every way—taller, faster, always ready with a dare. But he also listened. Really listened. Telly liked that about him.

That Saturday, they were racing sticks down the water, yelling like kids too big for their voices. Derrick leapt across a mossy boulder, missed his landing, and tumbled into a bed of tall grass.

His scream split the air.

Telly froze.

Derrick rolled to his side, clutching his ankle. "Something bit me," he gasped.

Telly rushed over. Derrick's ankle was already swelling. Two puncture marks glistened dark red above his boot.

A rattlesnake, fat and coiled, hissed just feet away, then slithered into the underbrush.

Telly's mind raced. He remembered everything James had taught him about snakebites—and how little time they had.

Derrick was pale now, trembling.

"I—I don't feel good," he whispered.

Telly dropped to his knees. "It's okay. I'm gonna help you."

He didn't ask. He didn't think.

He laid both hands on Derrick's leg.

The warmth surged like a river breaking through a dam. It flowed down his arms, through his fingers, and into the wound.

Derrick stiffened. Then, slowly, his breathing calmed. The color returned to his face.

The swelling in his ankle faded before their eyes.

Derrick stared at him. "Telly... what was that?"

Telly pulled his hands away, shaking. "You can't tell anyone. Please. You have to promise."

Derrick sat up slowly. The pain was gone. "You just saved my life."

Telly nodded, barely whispering. "That's why you can't say anything."

Derrick looked at the creek, then back at his friend. "I swear. I won't tell a soul."

They sat for a long time in silence, water rushing past them.

That night, Telly lay on his back, staring at the ceiling.

He had done it.

The line they warned him never to cross was now behind him.

It wasn't just a family secret anymore. It was real—and it was out in the world.

TEN

A Shift in the Wind
Blue Ridge Mountains
1995

The morning after the bite, Telly expected things to feel different. But the sky was still blue, the wind still sharp, and Derrick still cracked the same jokes as they walked to the edge of the woods together. You'd never guess he'd almost died.

Derrick hadn't said a word about it. He didn't limp. He didn't glance at Telly strangely. It was as if the snakebite—and what happened after—was locked in a drawer, sealed and silent.

Still, Telly felt it. The weight of it. The change.

At home, things stayed calm, but his thoughts grew louder. He couldn't stop replaying it—the speed of the venom, the heat in his palms, the way Derrick looked at him afterward.

What if it hadn't worked?

What if someone had seen?

A few days later, Telly heard voices in the kitchen.

"Got a call from the school board," James said. "They've been asking again. Wondering why we're still homeschooling."

"They know what we told them last year," Marianne said. "He's thriving here."

"It's getting harder to dodge," James said. "He's not a baby anymore. They're going to press it."

Telly leaned against the wall in the hallway, listening.

"You think it's time?" Marianne asked softly.

James didn't answer right away. "I think... if he's going to be in the world, we better prepare him for it."

That evening, Marianne sat beside Telly by the fireplace.

"Your father and I have been talking," she said. "About letting you spend more time in town. School, maybe. Or something like it."

Telly turned to her, eyes wide. "Why?"

"Because hiding forever isn't the same as being safe," she said. "And we think you might need to learn how to live among people who don't know. Not yet."

He didn't speak—just gave a slow nod, unsure if the tightness in his chest was fear or something closer to anticipation.

Outside, the wind picked up, rattling the trees.

Something was coming.

He could feel it in his bones.

James R. Baldwin

ELEVEN

Into the Fold
Blue Ridge Mountains
1996

Three weeks later, Telly stood outside the small town library, staring up at its red brick façade. The wind tugged at his sleeves, but his hands stayed in his pockets. His parents flanked him on either side, both silent.

It wasn't school. Not yet. But it was close.

The local librarian, Ms. Galloway, had agreed to let Telly join her weekly reading circle and afternoon writing club—an informal way to ease him into the presence of other kids without the weight of enrollment forms or school board scrutiny.

Inside, warm yellow lamps lit the wood-paneled room. Five other children sat on beanbags and mismatched chairs, each with a book in hand or a pencil between their fingers.

Telly stepped inside, heart thudding.

The afternoon passed in slow waves. He kept mostly to himself, answering questions only when Ms. Galloway called on him. But he noticed things: a boy with an inhaler who coughed when the heat kicked on, a girl with a bandage on her wrist, another with a heavy limp.

And he noticed something else—his hands tingled more here. The hum beneath his skin stronger.

He clenched his fists and focused on his notebook.

But one of the kids—Leah, the girl with the bandage on her wrist—noticed.

During the snack break, while the others huddled around the cookie tray, she approached quietly. "Hey," she said, her voice cautious. "Are you new?"

"Yeah," Telly said. "First time."

She nodded. "You were really quiet. Like... not shy, just listening."

"I guess I do that a lot."

Leah shifted, then held out her wrist. The bandage was loose. Beneath it, red marks traced across her skin—thin, deliberate lines.

"My mom says it's from my eczema. But that's not true."

Telly blinked. "Why are you telling me?"

She looked down, then back at him. "I don't know. You just seemed… different."

He didn't touch her. He wanted to. The warmth sparked in his fingertips like a match waiting to catch.

But he held it back.

"I hope it gets better," he said quietly.

She studied him. Then nodded. "Me too."

Leah grabbed his hand, only for a second, and walked away.

And Telly sat there, hands in his lap, the gift silent but heavy—like a truth trying to get out.

Afterward, as they walked home, James asked, "How was it?"

Telly shrugged. "Different. But good."

Marianne smiled. "You did something brave today."

"I didn't do anything," Telly muttered.

"Yes, you did," she said. "You entered the world. That matters."

That night, Telly stared at the ceiling again, but it wasn't fear that stirred in his chest.

It was the question he had begun to ask more often: What am I supposed to do with this?

And just beneath it, quieter but stronger: When?

James R. Baldwin

TWELVE

The Spark of Suspicion
Blue Ridge Mountains
1997

The next week, Telly returned to the library. The others were friendly enough, but Leah gave him a small nod as he entered—a silent acknowledgment of their shared secret.

As the kids settled into beanbags and pulled out their journals, Ms. Galloway noticed something.

Leah's wrist—once covered in gauze—was now completely bare. The red marks were gone.

"Leah," Ms. Galloway said gently, "your hand looks better. That cream must have really helped."

Leah hesitated, then nodded. "Yeah. I guess it did."

But the look in her eyes drifted to Telly.

And Ms. Galloway noticed.

That afternoon, a substitute helper from the local school—a retired nurse named Mrs. Enders—joined the group. She watched quietly from the back of the room as the kids read aloud. When Telly shared his writing—an innocent short story about a boy who could hear animals cry out in pain—her expression shifted.

After class, she pulled Ms. Galloway aside.

"That boy. Telly. Where's he from?"

"Lives on the east ridge," Galloway said. "Homeschooled. Why?"

Mrs. Enders frowned. "There's something about him. Can't explain it. Just... keep an eye open."

Later that week, Pastor Eli knocked on the Youngs' front door.

James let him in, surprised to see the pastor so somber.

"I heard a few whispers today," Eli said. "Someone's asking questions about your boy. Nothing direct, but curious."

James stiffened. "From who?"

"Someone at the library. Another at the school. All harmless—for now."

Marianne stepped in, her voice thin. "It's happening, isn't it?"

Eli nodded. "Eyes are opening. Slowly, but they are."

That night, the kitchen was silent.

"We may have to pull him out—again," James said, rubbing his temples.

"He's just starting to feel normal," Marianne whispered.

Telly, listening from the hallway, felt a cold twist in his chest.

He didn't want to run again. Not now.

Lying awake in the dark, eyes fixed on the ceiling, a strange sensation crept over him.

 It was pain

—but not his own. It came from somewhere else, far off and weighty, like a storm pressing at the edge of his thoughts. And it was calling to him.

James R. Baldwin

THIRTEEN

The Pull
Blue Ridge Mountains
1998

Telly woke before dawn. The sensation hadn't left. It had only grown stronger—like a whisper behind his ribs. A hum, steady and low, pulsing through his skin. He didn't know where it came from. Only that someone, somewhere, was hurting.

He dressed quickly, pulling on boots and a jacket. The house was silent, his parents still asleep.

He slipped out the back door and into the woods.

The cold bit at his face, but the pull guided him. Not like a sound or a scent—but a direction. A weight that grew lighter or heavier as he turned. It led him deeper into the forest than he'd ever gone.

He crossed the creek. Climbed the ridge. And there—beneath a fallen tree at the edge of a ravine—he found him.

A man. Mid-thirties. Pale. Barely breathing.

His leg was pinned under a heavy branch, twisted badly. One arm was scraped and raw, his face marked with blood and dried dirt.

Telly froze.

This wasn't an animal. This wasn't Derrick or Leah. This was a stranger.

He stepped closer, heart hammering.

The man moaned faintly.

Telly dropped to his knees. "Sir? Can you hear me?"

No answer. Only a shallow breath.

Telly placed one hand on the man's shoulder, the other on his leg. The warmth surged immediately. But this time it wasn't just healing—it was weight. Pressure. Like pouring from a vessel already half full.

His whole body tensed as the man's injuries began to fade. Bone aligned. Wounds closed. Bruises faded from purple to yellow to nothing.

The man stirred. Eyes fluttered open.

"Who..." he whispered. "Are you...?"

Telly pulled his hands away and stood.

"I'm sorry," he said. "I have to go."

And he ran.

By the time the man fully came to, the woods were empty.

But the pain was gone.

And he would remember one thing clearly: a boy. Blond. Barely twelve. Kneeling in the light between the trees.

A miracle.

By noon, the town would be whispering: someone had been found in the woods. Alive. Healed.

And no one could explain why.

FOURTEEN

The Rumor Mill
Blue Ridge Mountains
1998

By the next morning, half the town had heard about the man in the ravine. The official story, as told in hushed tones at the diner, was simple: a visiting hiker had been found by a search crew. His injuries were extensive. And then... they weren't.

"Nothing short of a miracle," said the sheriff's wife, pouring coffee refills. "Man says a kid found him. A boy with blond hair."

"Blond kid?" muttered an older man. "Sounds like James Young's boy. They homeschool, don't they?"

Others chimed in. "Wasn't there talk about that Young boy and that girl—Leah—at the library? She got better awful fast too."

Ms. Galloway didn't say anything. But her hand paused just slightly as she stamped books behind the counter.

At the clinic, Nurse Enders mentioned the hiker's recovery to Dr. Lena Cartwright, who happened to be visiting for research on rural health cases.

"Healing that fast? Impossible," Lena said, intrigued. "What did he say happened again?"

"Claims a kid healed him in the woods," Enders replied. "Sounds crazy, I know. But the man was near death, and now he's walking."

Dr. Cartwright wrote it down in her notebook.

She had heard similar stories before.

Back at the Youngs' home, James read the local paper twice. There was no mention of Telly. But the tone of the story... the language... it hit too close.

"We have to talk to him," James said to Marianne.

"He didn't tell us because he was trying to help," she replied quietly. "But this—it's getting too big."

In the next room, Telly stood by the window, staring toward the woods.

Something had changed.

And he knew—they were starting to see him.

James R. Baldwin

FIFTEEN

Held Back
Blue Ridge Mountains
2000

It happened during the town's Spring Jubilee. The festival was small, just booths and music at the park square, but the whole town turned out. Telly came with his parents, sticking close to their sides. The air smelled of kettle corn and roasted meat. Music played from the gazebo stage.

Marianne had just handed Telly a soda when the scream came.

A child had fallen from the stage steps. A little girl—six, maybe seven—lay still on the concrete, her arm twisted unnaturally.

People rushed over. A crowd formed fast.

Telly felt the pulse in his hands. The warmth, the unmistakable pull.

He stepped forward.

James caught his arm.

"Not here," he said firmly.

"But Dad, she's—"

"Not. Here."

Marianne stepped in beside them, eyes wide but steady. "You can't. Not in front of all these people."

The girl's mother cried out as the ambulance siren began to echo through the valley.

Telly's fists clenched. The pull burned in his chest, begging him to move. But he didn't.

He watched. Helpless.

The EMTs arrived within minutes. The girl was taken away, crying but conscious.

The next day, the story spread—but quietly.

People had seen the Young family nearby. Someone said Telly looked like he wanted to help but didn't. Others shrugged it off.

"If he was some miracle kid, wouldn't he have done something?"

Just like that, the talk slowed. Suspicion dulled. The town exhaled.

Back home, Telly sat alone on the porch steps.

Marianne joined him with a blanket and sat quietly beside him.

"You did the right thing," she whispered.

"I didn't do anything," he said.

She looked at him gently. "Sometimes doing nothing takes more strength than doing everything."

Telly didn't answer. His hands still burned.

He wondered if they always would.

That night, James and Marianne sat in their bedroom, the door half-shut. Their voices were soft, but the tension made them sharper than usual.

"We bought time," James said. "But that's all it is. Time."

Marianne sighed. "We can't live like this forever. He's getting older. The gift's getting stronger."

James stared out the window. "And the world's getting closer."

In his room, Telly lay awake, watching the shadows stretch across his ceiling.

For the first time, he questioned whether hiding was protecting anyone at all.

James R. Baldwin

SIXTEEN

The Woman in the Church
Blue Ridge Mountains
2001

Two Sundays later, the Youngs sat in their usual pew at the back of the small wooden church. Pastor Eli's sermon was gentle and measured, the kind that washed over the congregation like warm rain.

Telly fidgeted less now during services. He liked listening to Eli, even when he didn't fully understand the message. Today, it was about Jonah—about running from a calling.

"Sometimes," Eli said, "it's not the storm that finds us. It's the calling we're afraid to face."

James and Marianne exchanged a glance.

After the service, people lingered outside, chatting in small clusters.

That's when she approached.

A woman Telly didn't recognize—late forties, well-dressed, with tired eyes and a slow, deliberate way of moving—stepped toward them.

"Excuse me," she said softly. "Are you the Young family?"

"Yes," James replied, guarded.

"My name is Grace Halstead. I'm staying with my sister just outside town. I heard something—about the man who was found in the woods. The one who shouldn't have survived."

Telly's stomach twisted.

Grace's eyes locked on his. "Was that you?"

Before he could answer, Marianne stepped forward. "We've heard the stories too, ma'am. Just rumors."

Grace nodded slowly, not pressing. "Of course. I understand."

But she didn't move.

"I have a daughter," she added after a moment. "She's sick. Very sick. The kind no doctor knows what to do with. We've tried everything."

James' expression hardened. "I'm sorry to hear that."

Grace smiled, but it was thin and tired. "I don't believe in accidents. Just thought—if the stories were true…"

She turned to go, but paused.

"If you change your minds, we'll be here through the summer."

She walked away.

Telly's hands were already starting to warm.

And this time, they weren't the only ones who noticed.

SEVENTEEN

Grace
Blue Ridge Mountains
2001

Grace Halstead had once been a pediatric nurse. For over fifteen years, she'd worked rotating shifts in the ER at a children's hospital in Charlotte. It was the kind of job that left permanent marks—not always visible, but always there. She had learned how to hold the hand of a child in pain and how to smile through heartbreak. She had watched life begin and end in the same breath.

Grace had never believed in miracles. Not then.

She believed in charts. In vitals. In protocols and second opinions. She believed in catching symptoms early and keeping your voice steady when you delivered impossible news to grieving parents. Hope, to her, was always best kept in small doses—like morphine.

Then came Emily.

Her daughter had been born during a blizzard, the kind that shut down highways and bent pine trees to the ground. The ambulance barely made it in time. Emily arrived early—too early. She was fragile, almost translucent, and so quiet the room held its breath waiting for her first cry.

The doctors didn't mince words. "She may not make it through the week."

But she did.

She made it through the week.

Then the month.

Then a year.

It was a different kind of miracle, Grace thought. Not loud or dazzling—just defiant. Emily was small, but she had a grip that could make your finger ache, and eyes that tracked every sound like the world itself was a puzzle she was determined to solve.

But the years that followed weren't kind.

By the time Emily was six, her legs began to betray her. She'd fall while walking, drop toys without realizing it. Her voice became slower, her fingers unsteady. The diagnosis came quietly, delivered in a neurologist's office filled with pastel wallpaper and hollow words.

A degenerative neurological disorder. One so rare it didn't have a proper name—just a string of numbers and letters. A code. A curse.

"Her body will outgrow her," they said. "Her nerves won't keep up."

They said it clinically, but Grace heard what they meant: There is no cure. There is no path. Only delay.

Now thirteen, Emily spent her days in a wheelchair with a plaid blanket across her lap. Her speech was slow, her hands curled from muscle tightness, and every movement was effort. But her mind? Still razor sharp. She read voraciously. She asked questions no adult could answer easily. And every once in a while, when no one was looking, she still smiled with that same stubborn light she had on day one.

Grace had fought like hell.

She burned through every savings account. She chased every trial, every specialist, every whisper of a breakthrough. At some point, she stopped counting how many hospitals they'd seen. She moved in with her sister in the quiet Blue Ridge hills—not because she was giving up, but because she was tired of being chased by false hope.

She came to rest.

To breathe.

To stop chasing ghosts.

Until she heard about the man in the woods.

Not from the news. Not from any official source.

From Leah's mother—whose daughter's wrist healed overnight. From the mailman, who mentioned a boy with a stare like ice and hands like fire. From two unrelated sources in the span of one week, both whispering the same name: Young.

She didn't believe it. Not at first.

But something in her shifted.

She didn't go to church that Sunday for God. She didn't go to hear a sermon or sing hymns. She went with a question in her chest that she didn't dare say out loud.

When she saw the boy—blond, silent, too still for his age—she froze.

He was sitting in the second row. Hands folded. Eyes down.

But when he looked up—just once—the room fell away.

There was something in his gaze. Something that saw her—not just her face, but the worry carved deep beneath it. The ache she carried in every breath. And in that moment, something stirred.

Not hope.

Not yet.

But something more dangerous.

Belief.

James R. Baldwin

EIGHTEEN

The Choice
Blue Ridge Mountains
2001

That evening, James locked the front door early.

The sun hadn't fully set, but the light inside the house dimmed anyway—as if the walls themselves understood what kind of night it would be. Shadows stretched longer than they should have. Even the creak of the floorboards felt cautious.

Marianne moved quietly in the kitchen. She set a plate in front of Telly—roast chicken, green beans, mashed potatoes—but it sat untouched. The steam rose for a moment, then faded, curling into the hush that hung between them like fog.

Telly stared down at the plate. His shoulders were tight. Still. His fork untouched.

No one spoke for a long time.

Finally, James cleared his throat and broke the silence. "We're not going to visit that woman."

Telly didn't look up. "She didn't ask us to."

"No," James said evenly. "But you felt it. I saw it on your face at church."

Marianne sat down across from them, her hands folded so tightly her knuckles had gone white. Her voice was low but clear. "She's desperate, Telly. And desperate people get loud when they think they've found hope."

Telly raised his eyes to meet hers. "What if I could help her daughter?"

James's jaw tightened. "And what if someone sees you?" he said. "What if the girl walks again and her doctors can't explain it? What happens when her story spreads further than this town? What happens when they start asking who made it happen?"

"She's dying," Telly said. His voice didn't rise, but the weight behind it was louder than shouting. "And we're sitting here talking about rumors."

He looked at both of them now—his parents, the only people who knew him and still couldn't agree on what to do with him.

Marianne reached across the table, her touch tentative but full of love. "We're trying to protect you, Telly. Not from what you can do—but from what the world will do to you when they find out."

Telly slowly pulled his hands back.

He stood.

"Maybe it's not about me."

He turned and walked out of the room, his footsteps quiet on the wood floor.

Neither of them followed.

The rest of the night unfolded in silence.

James sat in his usual chair by the fireplace, staring into the flickering flames. He hadn't lit the fire for warmth—it was too early in the season for that—but for company.

The light danced across his face, highlighting the lines that had deepened over the last year. He didn't drink. He didn't pace. He just sat, as if the fire might give him an answer he hadn't been able to find on his own.

"She's not going to stop asking," he said finally, voice barely above a whisper.

Marianne stood nearby, her arms crossed as she watched the same fire. "No," she said softly. "And I don't think he's going to stop hearing."

In his room, Telly sat at the window, knees drawn up to his chest.

The stars blinked through the trees—sharp and clear. He knew every constellation above these hills. He used to name them with his mother when he was younger. Back when life felt simpler, when his hands were only meant for catching frogs or drawing pictures in the dirt.

Now, those same hands had done something else.

Something more.

And as he looked down at his palms, calm and still in his lap, the ache in his chest refused to fade.

Not guilt. Not fear.

Something deeper.

The weight of knowing you could act—and choosing not to.

For now.

NINETEEN

Breaking Point
Blue Ridge Mountains
2001

The next morning, Telly was gone. His bed was made, his boots missing. James found the back door unlocked, the morning frost on the handle barely disturbed.

They searched the trail behind the cabin first. Then the logging road. Then the hollow near the creek.

But James already knew where he'd gone.

Grace Halstead stood in the doorway, stunned, as the boy she'd met at church appeared on her sister's porch just after sunrise.

His hair was damp with mist, eyes steady, voice quiet.

"Can I see her?"

Grace blinked back emotion. "Does your family know you're here?"

He didn't answer.

She let him in.

Emily lay in a small bedroom off the hallway, her face pale, eyes heavy-lidded but aware. Her breathing was shallow, her limbs curled in from months of stiffness.

Telly stepped to the bed and knelt.

He took her hand.

He closed his eyes.

The warmth came—not just strong, but complete. Like everything in him had been waiting for this exact moment.

Grace watched from the doorway, tears tracking silently down her cheeks.

Emily stirred. Her hands uncurled. Her chest rose deeper. Her eyes opened—clearer than they'd been in weeks.

Telly stood, shaky but still.

He turned to go.

Grace whispered, "Thank you."

He didn't speak.

But he nodded.

An hour later, he walked through the back door of his home.

James and Marianne were waiting.

They didn't shout.

They didn't scold.

They just looked at him—tired, afraid, and proud all at once.

And James finally said what none of them had dared to:

"It's out now. We can't put it back.

James R. Baldwin

TWENTY

Echoes
Blue Ridge Mountains
2001

The news spread like a breeze through tall grass—gentle at first, barely noticeable. Then, everywhere.

Three days after Telly's quiet visit to the Halstead home, Emily was seen walking through the church garden. Her mother held her hand, guiding her slowly beneath the dogwoods. No wheelchair. No tremors. No slack muscles or labored breath. Her steps were steady, uncertain like a foal's, but strong.

She smiled.

And that was what undid the silence.

"She said she just got better overnight," the Sunday school teacher whispered in the fellowship hall, half-believing it herself. "Said she woke up and just… stood up."

"Must've been one of those rare recoveries," someone else offered over coffee and hymnals. "The kind science can't explain but tries to."

But Alder Bend had never needed much to turn a whisper into a wave.

And it wasn't long before Grace's sister let something slip at the grocery store, right between the canned green beans and instant rice.

"A boy," she said casually to the cashier, barely even lowering her voice. "She said a boy came to the house. Before the change."

That was all it took.

By that evening, the name Young resurfaced.

Whispers passed between families like shared secrets.

Back at the Youngs' cabin, the quiet began to warp.

The phone rang twice that week—each time after dinner. No voice. Just silence. Then a soft click.

James unplugged it by the third call.

A local reporter from the county paper drove past the house slowly—once in the morning, once in the evening. The second time, he paused at the mailbox, camera on the passenger seat. That was enough to make James step onto the porch with his arms crossed and a look that needed no words.

At the library, Ms. Galloway noticed something else— Leah, sitting by the window, her gaze locked on Telly as he crossed the street. Not curious. Not afraid.

Studying him.

Rumors returned. Louder now.

Not just in hushed church corners or between friends.

In notes.

In folded slips of paper left on their porch, slid through the cracks in the church pew, tucked between library books.

Voices emerged in the least expected places—behind gas pumps, outside the post office, whispered in the hallway after service.

"Can you help my daughter?"

"My brother is sick."

"I'm not asking for a miracle. Just a conversation."

They weren't threats.

They were pleas.

People who'd stopped hoping started asking.

Telly read every note. Every one of them.

He didn't reply.

He didn't throw them away, either.

He sat by the fire most nights, his hands curled in his lap, the stack of papers growing slowly in a drawer beside his bed. The ache inside him hadn't faded.

If anything, it had multiplied.

This wasn't a secret anymore.

This wasn't a story told only within four walls.

They knew now.

And some—more than a few—had started to believe.

TWENTY-ONE

The Visitors
Blue Ridge Mountains
2001

By the end of the week, the knocks began. The first came just after dusk—a man from the next county, truck still running in the drive. His daughter sat in the front seat, thin and pale, wrapped in a blanket. Her cough echoed faintly through the open window.

The man stood on the porch, eyes sunken, voice low. "They say someone here helped a girl… that it was real."

James met him at the door, boots planted, arms folded. "We're not the people you're looking for."

The man didn't argue. He just stared a moment longer, nodded once, and left without another word.

The second came two nights later.

A woman in scrubs, circles under her eyes, a hospital badge still clipped to her collar. She'd driven all night from a few towns over. Her husband was dying of pancreatic cancer.

She didn't plead. But her eyes—wide, raw—spoke louder than any words.

Marianne stood in the doorway, hand on the frame.

"I'm sorry," she said gently, "but please... don't come back."

The woman didn't move at first. Then she turned, climbed into her car, and disappeared into the dark.

But they kept coming.

By the fourth knock, no one even stood. The door stayed closed. The lights stayed dim. But the silence in the house grew heavier by the day.

It followed them through dinner. Lingered in every room. Settled behind every word left unsaid.

One night, they sat around the kitchen table, the only sound the faint clink of a spoon against porcelain.

James finally broke the quiet. "We're going to have to say something. Silence isn't working anymore."

Marianne sighed. "But what? If we lie, they'll see through it. If we tell the truth... he'll be overwhelmed."

Telly looked up from his untouched bowl. His voice was calm. Tired. Certain.

"Then maybe we say something that's true… but not everything."

James raised an eyebrow, leaning forward. "Go on."

Telly met his eyes. "We say I helped someone. But not that I can help everyone. Not that I understand how it works. Not that I even control it."

Marianne looked at him carefully, her face creased with worry. "Are you sure you're ready for that?"

"I'm not sure of anything," Telly admitted. "But they're not going to stop coming. And I can't hide from them… or from myself."

James nodded slowly, gaze shifting to the old typewriter in the corner.

"Then tomorrow," he said, "we'll write something. And we'll let the town read it."

James R. Baldwin

TWENTY-TWO

The Letter
Blue Ridge Mountains
2001

The next morning, James sat at the kitchen table with a legal pad in front of him. Telly and Marianne stood nearby as he wrote, slowly, carefully—pausing after every sentence.

They read it together when he finished:

To the people of Alder Bend,

Our family has lived quietly for many years. Recently, some of you have seen or heard things that may seem extraordinary. We understand your questions.

What we can tell you is this: our son, Telly, has helped people. Not always. Not everyone. But when he can, and when it feels right, he does. We don't claim to understand it completely ourselves.

We ask for your respect. Your patience. And most of all, your privacy. This is not a miracle to be demanded, but something we are still learning how to carry.

We love this town. And we trust that love will be returned in understanding.

— James, Marianne, and Telly Young

James printed a dozen copies and took them into town. One for the library. One for the church. One for the bulletin board at the gas station.

By nightfall, every diner, store, and front porch in Alder Bend had heard about it.

Some scoffed. Others nodded. A few were moved to tears.

But the stream of visitors slowed.

And for the first time in weeks, the Young family sat through dinner without a knock on the door.

James R. Baldwin

TWENTY-THREE

The Town Listens
Blue Ridge Mountains
2001

Alder Bend wasn't a place for secrets. Not really. Not with a single stoplight, two diners, and a church that hosted both weddings and weekly pancake breakfasts. News here didn't break—it seeped, spreading like coffee across a linen tablecloth.

So when the letter from the Young family went public, people didn't just read it—they dissected it.

By sunrise the next day, a copy of the note was taped inside the window of Sadie's Diner. Before lunch, three people had snapped photos of it with shaky hands and whispered voices. By sunset, someone had printed twenty more and left them on the counter at

Holman's General Store, beside the register where the gum and hunting licenses were kept.

At church that Sunday, Pastor Eli stepped to the pulpit and didn't mention Telly by name. He didn't have to.

He simply opened his Bible and spoke about the gifts we don't ask for. The burdens that feel too heavy. The ways in which miracles, too, demand sacrifice.

Some nodded. Some looked away.

Mrs. Donnelly wept quietly into her handkerchief.

After the service, the fellowship hall buzzed louder than the coffee machine. People didn't speak in accusations, just... wonder.

"Did you see her? Emily Halstead? Walking?"

"My sister said Grace looked ten years younger just from smiling again."

"God gives signs," someone whispered. "And sometimes He gives messengers."

And then—"It's unnatural," came a firmer voice from the back. "No boy should be able to do that. It isn't right."

Pastor Eli stepped in gently, not to silence, but to soothe. "Whether we understand it or not, fear is no compass for truth."

Down by the river, a group of teenagers gathered on the old dock with soda cans and loose talk.

"Did he really heal someone?"

"My brother said he saw the dog. Was dying one day, chasing squirrels the next."

"He's not even weird. Just quiet."

A few laughed, trying to shake off the unease. But even laughter sounded different now.

At the hardware store, James Holman—owner, war vet, lifelong skeptic—stood behind the counter and watched people come in just to stare at the letter.

"Don't know what they expect it to say," he muttered, folding his arms.

But when someone asked him directly if he believed it, he didn't say no.

He just said, "Kid always looked like he carried more than his size."

And at home, behind drawn curtains, the Young family waited.

Marianne cleaned a counter that didn't need cleaning. James stood at the window, arms crossed, eyes on the driveway.

Telly sat at the table, staring at the blank page in front of him.

He didn't feel relief.

He didn't feel exposed.

He felt something deeper—like the whole town had exhaled at once, and now everyone was holding their breath, waiting to see what he'd do next.

He reached for a pen, not to write another letter—but because he couldn't sit still.

Because the silence of Alder Bend wasn't quiet anymore.

It was listening.

TWENTY-FOUR

The Stillness Before
Blue Ridge Mountains
2001

The world held its breath.

Snow had fallen the night before, not heavy, but thick enough to blanket Alder Bend in silence. Tree limbs were dusted white, fences half-disguised, roofs softened by frost. It was the kind of morning that made noise feel intrusive.

In town, the diner opened late. Sadie turned on the coffee pot but didn't flip the radio on. She moved more slowly, eyes drifting toward the frosted windows more often than usual.

The post office didn't unlock its doors until noon.

No one complained.

Even the church remained quiet, its bell silent, its parking lot mostly undisturbed.

It was as if the whole town had sensed something shifting—an invisible wind, a ripple before the stone drops.

✳✳✳

At the edge of the woods, the Youngs' cabin stood like a memory. Smoke no longer rose from the chimney. No fresh tracks marred the snow leading up to the porch. But behind the stillness, something stirred.

Inside, Telly sat at the kitchen table, his coat still on. The letter they had written weeks ago was folded in front of him, edges soft from handling.

His breath fogged faintly in the cold. The fire hadn't been lit.

He wasn't sure why.

Maybe he didn't want comfort today.

He traced the edges of the paper with one finger. He could feel it—that tension again. Not panic. Not dread.

Anticipation.

Like a wave rolling in from a long way off.

Down in town, people whispered again.

They didn't gather—not quite. But they lingered longer at the store, asked one more question than necessary at the register.

"Has anyone seen the boy?"

"He hasn't been at church."

"Grace's daughter still walks like nothing ever happened."

Some spoke with reverence. Others with doubt. But all of them spoke.

And that was the change.

The story was no longer about a single healing. It was about possibility. About what might happen next.

Telly finally stood and walked to the window. The trees were bare but beautiful—limbs like bones stretching toward the sky.

He closed his eyes and listened.

There it was.

A hum. Not in the air, but in him. Steady. Rising.

Something was coming.

Not a person.

Not a moment.

A turning.

And somewhere, somehow, a choice was already unfolding.

TWENTY-FIVE

The Breaking News
Blue Ridge Mountains
2001

It came on a Tuesday morning—unassuming at first. The kind of morning where frost clung stubbornly to the windowpanes and the hills breathed thin plumes of mist into the cold air. Telly was outside, helping James organize the tool shed. The metal tools clanged softly, echoing in the crisp silence.

Then came the knock—not on the front door, but the kitchen window.

Inside, Marianne stood pale-faced, the cordless phone still in her hand.

"You need to see this," she said.

They followed her into the living room, where the soft hum of the old television already filled the space. The screen flickered with the image of a regional news anchor, crisp in her delivery, with a photo of Grace Halstead and Emily in the corner.

"...a small Appalachian town where residents are claiming a young girl made a miraculous recovery after months in a wheelchair. Sources say a boy may have been involved."

The name wasn't spoken.

But it didn't have to be.

Telly's stomach twisted. Marianne's hand reached for the armrest. James stood like stone.

Then came the footage.

Emily—walking. Talking. Laughing.

Her steps were sure. Her body, once curled in pain, moved freely. The camera zoomed in on Grace's tearful embrace, a moment captured with enough weight to shatter silence.

Telly's photo appeared next.

Not a name. Just the school picture from a community flier—his blond hair and unreadable eyes staring from the corner of the screen.

Then the voice again, cutting through the still air like a scalpel:

"The town of Alder Bend now finds itself at the center of growing speculation. Who is Telly Young? And how did this happen?"

James turned off the TV.

The screen went black, but the moment lingered like smoke in the room.

No one spoke. The only sound was the ticking of the wall clock, slow and hollow.

Outside, the wind shifted—rattling loose frost from the porch railing. The air seemed different now.

Like something had cracked open.

And stillness no longer belonged to them.

James R. Baldwin

TWENTY-SIX

The Watchers
Blue Ridge Mountains
2001

The first sign was small.

Just a car, parked at the edge of the church lot. It didn't belong to anyone they knew. Out-of-state plates. Dusty. Engine still warm when James walked past after Sunday service.

The man inside never made eye contact.

He just looked down at a map he didn't seem to read.

Three days later, the phone line crackled every time they answered it. Not with voices—just static. Sometimes it hissed. Sometimes it clicked.

James called the phone company. They said the line looked fine.

Marianne started unplugging it at night.

Then came the figures. Not often. Not every night. But enough.

Shadowed silhouettes parked just past the treeline. Pale flashes of binoculars. The faint orange flare of cigarettes in the dark.

They never came close. Never spoke.

But they were always there.

Watching.

James kept the rifle closer now.

He hadn't carried it since the last hunt with Telly. It felt heavier. Less like a tool, more like a warning.

Marianne moved like someone expecting a knock that wouldn't be gentle.

And Telly? He started waking up in the middle of the night. Always at the same time—3:17 a.m. Heart pounding. Ears ringing.

Sometimes, he swore he heard footsteps just outside the house.

He stopped mentioning it.

He didn't want to make it real.

By the end of the week, someone left a note on the porch.

No envelope. No name.

Just a folded page.

"People are watching. They want to know. Keep your boy inside."

James burned it in the sink.

But the smell lingered long after the smoke was gone.

That night, Telly stood at the kitchen window, staring out into the trees.

"I feel them," he whispered. "Even when I can't see them."

James stood beside him. Silent.

Marianne wrapped a blanket tighter around her shoulders, as if that could block out more than the cold.

No one asked who "they" were.

Because deep down, they already knew.

They weren't just dealing with curiosity anymore.

This was interest.

This was intent.

The watchers were no longer outside the circle.

They were drawing closer.

James R. Baldwin

TWENTY-SEVEN

The Line
Blue Ridge Mountains
2001

The next day, a black SUV appeared at the end of their long gravel drive.

No logos. No plates they recognized. The windows were tinted too dark to see inside. It didn't move once it parked—just sat idling, quiet and deliberate.

A man stepped out.

He wore a charcoal suit and carried a clipboard, but no badge was visible. His eyes scanned the house—not searching, just absorbing, like he already knew everything he needed to. He didn't approach. Didn't knock. Didn't wave.

He waited.

James watched from the porch, arms crossed. Ten full minutes passed before he moved. He walked slowly down the drive, every step crunching over the gravel like a warning. Telly stood behind the living room curtain, breath held, watching them face each other in the early light.

No handshake.

No smile.

Just a few clipped words exchanged across a line that felt suddenly permanent.

James's shoulders tightened as the man said something—Telly couldn't hear what, but the expression on his father's face told him enough. A crease formed at the corner of James's jaw, the same one Telly had only ever seen in arguments or war stories.

Then, without a nod or gesture, the man turned, walked back to his SUV, and drove away—dust kicking up behind the wheels, fading into the morning mist.

James came inside and locked the door behind him. Slowly. Firmly.

He didn't speak at first. Just stood in the foyer like he was waiting for the weight of it all to settle.

Finally, he said, "Government."

Marianne froze in the kitchen, hand still holding a dish towel. "Which agency?"

"They didn't say. Just that they're... interested."

She covered her mouth, eyes wide, breath catching in her throat.

Telly sat down hard at the kitchen table. His hands trembled, not from fear exactly, but from something colder. More final.

That night, after dinner, James went out to the back shed. When he returned, he carried something wrapped in a towel—old and heavy. He placed it on the kitchen table and slowly unwrapped it.

A metal lockbox.

Inside were passports. Birth certificates. Rolls of cash sealed in plastic bags. One of Telly's old photos, clipped to a second ID with a different last name.

A plan.

James looked across the table, his voice low and even. "We're not running. Not yet. But if they come for you—if they try to take you—we don't stay here."

Marianne said nothing. She just nodded and placed her hand on top of the box like it was sacred.

Telly looked between them, the ache behind his eyes pulsing.

He didn't want to leave.

Not the trees. Not the creek. Not the worn floorboards of the house that had held every version of him since birth. Not the people in town who had just started to see him—not as a threat, but as something else.

But he knew what this was.

He'd seen it in the way the man never made eye contact.

He'd heard it in the silence after the SUV vanished.

Sometimes, understanding isn't enough.

Sometimes, the world draws a line before you're ready.

And now it was up to him to decide which side he stood on.

TWENTY-EIGHT

The Choice Repeated
Blue Ridge Mountains
2001

The letter arrived two days later, slipped beneath the front door sometime before sunrise. The envelope was plain. No return address. Just a single sheet of paper.

My name is Eliora. I'm thirteen. I don't want to be a story on the news. I just want to live.

If you're real, I believe you already know where I am.

Telly read it once. Then again.

He didn't know the girl. But he knew the name.

And he felt it—that pull. That ache. That certainty.

He packed a small bag.

This time, James didn't stop him. Marianne only hugged him longer than usual.

"Be smart," she said. "Be safe."

Telly nodded, then left without another word.

He found Eliora in a house on the far edge of town, hidden behind a rusted gate. Her aunt answered the door. No reporters. No cameras. Just a girl in a dark room with hollow cheeks and trembling hands.

Telly knelt beside her. Reached for her hand. And once again, gave everything he had.

He stumbled out into the yard afterward, heart racing, eyes damp. She was breathing easier. Sitting up. Smiling faintly.

He'd done it again.

But something felt wrong.

He turned back toward the road and saw the van.

Black. No markings.

A man stepped out. Then another.

He ran and hid in his father's shed.

That night, James and Marianne sat on the porch, waiting.

They never saw the van.

But they felt the crash.

And by morning, the news broke again—this time with names.

James and Marianne Young: found dead in a cabin fire.

Authorities seek missing son.

Believed to be connected to recent miracle cases.

Telly watched it all from a truck stop TV, hood up, backpack at his feet.

Alone now.

In hiding.

And for the first time, completely free.

James R. Baldwin

TWENTY-NINE

The New Name
Blue Ridge Mountains
2001

Three weeks after the fire, Telly was someone else. His hair was shorter. His clothes were thrifted and worn soft at the edges. He went by Luke now—Luke Davis—just another teenager working behind the counter at a run-down gas station outside Knoxville.

He spoke little. Smiled less. But he listened.

People talked when they thought no one was paying attention. And more than once, someone mentioned a healing they couldn't explain. A recovery they didn't deserve. A boy.

He stayed quiet. He stayed small.

But the ache never left.

And some nights, it burned.

He hadn't cried during the funeral. Hadn't even attended one.

It happened just after dusk.

James and Marianne had been sitting on the front porch, side by side in their weathered rocking chairs. Telly remembered that day vividly—cool air, golden light filtering through the trees, the scent of pine and tobacco rising as James smoked his pipe. It had been calm. Ordinary. Safe.

Until it wasn't.

The sound came first—a low roar tearing up the gravel road, engine whining like something wounded and wild. Then headlights. Too fast. Too straight. No curve of caution. No swerve of hesitation.

The black SUV exploded through the tree line and smashed through the porch like it wasn't there, wood shattering, chairs splintering, glass and bone and memory crushed beneath steel.

Then came the silence. And the smoke.

Telly hadn't seen it—he was out back in the shed—but he heard it. He ran. And when he turned the corner, what he saw never stopped replaying in his mind.

The cabin—cracked open. Walls sagging. Porch gone. The SUV's nose was buried halfway through the living room, the engine steaming like some mechanical beast out of breath. Debris scattered everywhere. A porch step rested in the bushes ten feet away. James's favorite mug was shattered in the grass.

And his parents... gone.

The authorities called it a tragic accident.

"Brake failure," the coroner said. "They wouldn't have felt a thing. Quick. Painless."

But Telly didn't believe that. Not really.

Because the SUV had no plates.

Because no one ever claimed it.

Because the driver was missing.

Gone.

And the more he thought about it, the more the scene twisted in his memory. He pictured the moment they realized—James rising from his chair, the quiet flicker of instinct too late to mean anything. Marianne's hand reaching for the door. Or each other.

He saw their faces. Not in fear—but in understanding.

They had always known something like this might happen.

That someone might come.

And deep down, Telly knew it too.

It wasn't brake failure.

It wasn't bad luck.

It was a message. Too many whispers. Too many coincidences.

They had protected him. Hidden him. And now they were gone.

Every night, he turned their final conversations over in his mind, searching for a missed clue. A final warning. A name someone never said.

But the silence offered no answers.

Only guilt.

And grief.

On his days off, he wandered the outskirts of town— quiet trails, overgrown fields, rusting barns with names long forgotten. He liked the forgotten places. No one asked questions there.

Once, he saw a woman crying in her car and almost knocked on the window. Her shoulders shook. Her face was buried in her hands.

He reached out.

Then stopped.

He didn't know who was watching anymore. Or what would happen if they found him again.

So he turned and walked away.

Not yet.

He was learning now. Learning how to blend. How to disappear.

How to listen deeper than he ever had.

Because he knew something now—something carved deep by loss:

He wasn't the only one who needed healing.

And he wasn't the only one being watched.

The Touch of Telly D. Young

James R. Baldwin

Part TWO

The Awakened

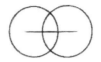

THIRTY

Signals

The first time he noticed it, he was sweeping the station lot. A symbol—two circles intersecting with a line through them—scratched lightly into the pump post. It hadn't been there the day before.

A week later, it showed up again.

This time on a sticky note taped to the back of the cooler. No words. Just the symbol.

Telly pocketed it and said nothing.

But something shifted in his gut.

Not fear. Not yet.

Recognition.

At night, he started dreaming again—faces he didn't know, voices he'd never heard. One word whispered over and over:

Awakened.

He didn't know what it meant.

Until the envelope arrived.

No stamp. No name. Just his new one, written in sharp, precise print:

Luke Davis.

Inside was a folded paper and a GPS coordinate. Nothing else.

But as soon as he touched it, the ache in his palms sparked again.

There was someone out there.

Someone like him.

Or worse—someone who wanted someone like him.

The Touch of Telly D. Young

James R. Baldwin

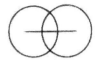

THIRTY-ONE

Coordinates
Ohio

Telly didn't sleep that night. He lay awake in the cramped apartment above the gas station, staring at the torn scrap of paper with the GPS coordinates scribbled in fading ink.

The pull in his chest throbbed like a second heartbeat.

By sunrise, he had packed his things—just a few clothes, some cash, and the map.

No goodbye. No note.

He walked ten miles before finding a bus heading north.

The coordinates led him to a wooded hill near a humming power station in Kentucky. Rusted towers loomed in the distance, buzzing faintly through the trees. There were no signs. No people. Just mud, pine needles, and the damp breath of winter rising from the forest floor.

Then he saw it—carved into a moss-covered rock near the tree line:

Two intersecting circles.

And beneath it, etched in small, sharp digits, another set of coordinates.

He didn't hesitate.

He followed.

Three days. Two rides. One quiet border town in Ohio.

He ate little. Slept less.

The final coordinates led him to an abandoned barn, leaning sideways against the weight of time and weather. The roof had caved in near the back. Vines strangled the outer walls. Wind rattled loose boards like bones in a forgotten grave.

It looked empty.

But something told him otherwise.

The hum was there again. Low. Steady. Alive.

He stepped inside.

And someone was waiting.

A girl—maybe sixteen. Pale, calm, and still. Her blond hair was chopped short, her arms crossed over a patched coat.

"You're late," she said.

Telly froze. "You know me?"

She nodded once. "You're one of us."

He took a step forward. "Us?"

She didn't smile. Just pointed to the ground.

There, drawn in white chalk across the barn floor, was a circle.

Inside it: five names.

His was one of them.

THIRTY-TWO

The Awakened

Her name was Sera. She didn't say where she was from, only that she'd been on the run since she was twelve. "Like you," she said, "I lost everything the moment I used it in front of the wrong person."

Telly sat in the dust, eyes on the circle.

The names were faded but readable. Sera's. His own. Three others:

Caleb. Noor. Ash.

"They're not all here," she said. "But we're connected. All of us. You felt it, didn't you? The pull. The signal."

Telly nodded slowly.

Sera handed him a folded piece of parchment—thicker than normal paper. It felt warm in his hand.

Inside were drawings. Maps. Symbols. Notes in strange handwriting.

"They call us the Awakened," Sera said. "And someone is collecting us. Some to protect. Some to exploit. No one knows how many are out there. But every time one of us uses our gift, they get closer."

Telly looked up. "Who?"

She hesitated. Then whispered:

"The ones who don't believe in healing. Only control."

A cold silence settled between them.

Outside the barn, the wind shifted.

Telly understood something now. He wasn't just being hunted.

He was part of a war that hadn't begun yet.

But it would.

THIRTY-THREE

Names in the Circle

Later that night, Telly sat with Sera near a broken window in the barn. The air smelled like damp straw and rust, but the silence between them had grown comfortable.

"Tell me about the others," he said.

Sera nodded. "They've all lost something. That's how it starts. The pain comes first. The gift wakes after."

She pointed to the first name in the circle.

James R. Baldwin

Caleb – "He's from Texas. Could feel sickness like a second skin. He used to sit in hospitals to be near people who were dying—said the pain made him calm. When he started healing with touch, the hospital called security. His mom got scared. Disappeared with him in the night. He's quiet, but loyal. He's seen what happens when people beg you to fix everything."

She traced the second.

Noor – "She is from London. Her family thought she was possessed. Not healing exactly—she sees the truth. Pain behind smiles. Lies in someone's heartbeat. They called her a witch. She escaped to a shelter and eventually found one of our signs. She does not trust easily."

Then, the third.

Ash – "No one knows where he came from. Rumor is he was raised off-grid. He can shut down pain—emotionally and physically. Just... silence. Useful when someone is dying. Dangerous if he is angry. He is the only one ever pushed back against the Circle."

Telly ran his fingers over his name.

"And me?" he asked.

Sera did not answer right away.

"You are the first one we did not find," she said softly. "You found us."

THIRTY-FOUR

Contact

The barn was still when Telly woke the next morning. Sera was gone, but her note remained. "Follow the marks. Caleb will find you first. Trust him."

Telly folded the note and slipped it into his jacket. The symbols on the map Sera had shown him still echoed in his mind—circles, lines, stars.

He knew this was no longer about hiding.

It was about finding the others.

And understanding what they were about to face.

He left the barn at first light.

The air was thick with fog, making the trees look like shadows from another world. Telly walked north, following the signs carved into tree bark and stones: the intersecting circles, small arrows, and once, the name "Caleb" scratched into a piece of bark with a crude arrow pointing left.

By dusk, he reached a clearing. A small, silent fire burned near the base of a fallen tree.

A boy sat beside it. Older than Telly by a few years. Shaved head. Worn jacket. He didn't look up.

"I figured you'd come," the boy said.

"Caleb?"

The boy nodded slowly, tossing a twig into the flame. "You're late."

Telly stepped into the light. "You're the second person who's said that to me."

Caleb glanced at him now. His eyes were tired but curious. "You feel it, don't you? The others? The pressure building?"

Telly nodded. "It never stops."

Caleb stood and extended a hand. "Then you're ready. Let's get you caught up."

Telly took it.

And with that, the next chapter began.

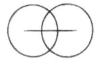

THIRTY-FIVE

Gathering Light

Caleb moved with quiet confidence, guiding Telly through a maze of forgotten trails and brush-choked paths that snaked beneath ancient trees. The forest was thick here—older, more untamed than anything Telly had walked through before. Roots twisted across the earth like veins, and branches clawed at his jacket as if trying to hold him back.

They didn't speak much. Caleb moved too fast for small talk, and Telly was too busy watching the shadows between the trees. He could feel the silence—not just the absence of sound, but the kind that warned you something was listening.

By morning, they crested a ridge and descended into a hollow swallowed by fog. At the center of it sat what looked like the skeleton of an old chapel—its stone bones slouched beneath a heavy canopy of vines. Ivy crept across shattered walls. The bell tower had long since collapsed, and shards of stained glass glittered like forgotten stars beneath the mossy floor.

It looked like time had tried to erase it.

But the place lived.

This was a safehouse.

Caleb pushed open the warped wooden door. The hinges groaned, then gave way.

Inside, the air was cool and quiet. Candlelight flickered against the stone walls, casting long shadows that danced across the floor. Blankets were rolled tight in corners, gear tucked neatly along the walls—everything had purpose. A solar-powered radio buzzed faintly from a small wooden table, sending out pulses of static like a heartbeat.

Near the window, a figure sat with her back half-turned.

She didn't rise.

But Telly felt her eyes land on him before he spoke a word.

Her hair was pulled back into a tight braid, and her posture was one of discipline, not comfort. The kind of stillness forged through years of waiting for the wrong thing to happen.

Her voice was sharp. Clipped.

"So, you're the boy everyone's whispering about," she said.

Telly hesitated, still adjusting to the shift from forest to sanctuary. "Depends who's whispering."

Caleb stepped forward and gave her a nod. "He's here. And he's not what the news made him out to be."

The girl stood, unfolding herself in one smooth motion. She was lean and compact, like someone who'd learned how to make herself smaller in rooms where she didn't feel safe—and had never quite unlearned it.

She walked slowly around Telly, eyes scanning him the way a tracker reads footprints.

"He better not be," she said, her voice low, dry.

Telly met her stare. "I didn't come here to be famous. I came because I had nowhere else."

There was a flicker then—just for a second—in her expression. A softening around the eyes, not quite trust, but the recognition of something familiar: that edge-of-nowhere desperation.

"Good," she said. "Because this isn't a shelter. It's a choice."

She turned back toward the window.

Caleb moved toward the far wall, pulling back a tarp that revealed a long table beneath.

It was covered with maps—faded and hand-marked—photos, scribbled notes, and red string connecting one place to another. Faces. Names. Circles. Stars. And Xs—too many Xs.

Telly stepped closer.

"This," Caleb said, gesturing over it all, "is everyone we know. Every Awakened who hasn't been taken. Or worse."

Telly stared.

The weight of it crashed down on him.

Cities. Forests. Underground facilities. Some names scratched out. Some marked with question marks.

This wasn't just a few people.

This was something vast.

A network. A war map.

And for the first time, he realized just how many were still out there. People like him.

And how far they had to go to reach them.

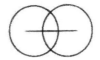

THIRTY-SIX

The Interrogator

Far from the safehouse's quiet ruins and candles, a sterile, windowless facility hummed with fluorescent light. Agent Victor Klemens sat across from a monitor, his expression unreadable. The screen showed grainy security footage of a barn in Ohio, with a boy entering and a girl waiting.

"Pause," he said.

The technician froze the frame. Klemens leaned forward, narrowing his eyes at the boy's outline.

He tapped a finger against the image.

"Telly Young. Still breathing."

Klemens wasn't new to this. He'd spent years in foreign intel, watching unstable leaders pretend to wield power. But this? These Awakened? They weren't pretending.

His desk was filled with files—photos, footage, and medical reports flagged as anomalies. The Young file alone was thicker than a phone book.

He picked up a page—the coroner's report from the cabin fire.

Empty casket. DNA inconclusive.

They hadn't gotten him.

Not yet.

He turned to the map on the wall. Pins scattered across states, lines connecting sightings, notes about Noor, Ash, and the girl from London who disappeared near a border.

"Activate Tier Two teams," he said. "Start with the one they'll protect. The healer."

The technician paused. "Sir, are we initiating extraction?"

Klemens smiled faintly.

"Not yet. We let them gather. Let them feel safe. Then… we learn what they're willing to lose."

James R. Baldwin

THIRTY-SEVEN

The Circle Fractures

Back at the safehouse, the tension was building. Noor had picked up on it first—the static in the air and the odd interference in their shortwave radio. Then came the silence: two safehouses no longer responding—one in upstate New York and the other outside Flagstaff.

"They've found someone," Noor said, pacing. "Or worse—they've taken one of us."

Telly stood by the map table, watching the blinking radio light fade.

Caleb folded his arms. "We need to assume we're compromised."

Noor shot him a look. "And go where? Underground again? Keep running until one of us vanishes, too?"

Telly raised his voice, calm but steady. "We can't split. Not now. That's what they want."

"I'd rather run than rot in one of their labs," Noor snapped. "You don't know what they're capable of."

"I know enough," Telly said. "And I know we're stronger together than hunted alone."

For a moment, no one spoke.

Then the door creaked.

A figure stepped inside—mud-covered, breathing hard.

It was Ash.

Everyone froze.

Ash didn't wait for greetings.

"They took Noor's contact in Colorado," he said. "Dragged him out of a shelter like it was nothing. They're escalating."

His eyes landed on Telly.

"They know you're alive. And now they know you're not alone."

The Touch of Telly D. Young

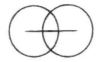

THIRTY-EIGHT

Ash

Ash tossed his pack onto the ground and sat against the wall like he owned the room. His eyes, dark and sharp, scanned each of them in turn.

"You've been playing it soft," he said. "Waiting. Watching. Hoping they'd leave us alone."

"We've been surviving," Noor shot back.

Ash smirked. "Surviving isn't enough anymore."

Caleb folded his arms. "Then what do you suggest?"

Ash reached into his coat and pulled out a small flash drive. "This. I took it off a field op van that rolled over trying to chase me down near St. Louis. It's encrypted, but someone on our side managed to pull some of it apart."

He dropped the drive onto the table. "Names. Coordinates. Experimental sites. They're not just hunting us. They're studying us. And they've already started building something to contain us."

Telly leaned forward. "What kind of something?"

"Facilities. Off-grid black sites. Places where people like us disappear."

Silence filled the chapel.

Ash's voice dropped. "You want to survive, we need to move. We need to gather. And we need to go dark. Completely. No more signals. No more safehouses. No more mercy."

Caleb looked at Telly.

Telly looked at the map.

The war had already started.

They were just late to the front lines.

James R. Baldwin

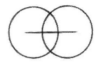

THIRTY-NINE

Visions in the Fire

That night, Telly couldn't sleep.

The fire had burned low, casting long, uneven shadows across the crumbling chapel walls. The others had drifted into uneasy rest—Noor curled beneath her jacket in the corner, Ash sitting upright with his back to the stone, Caleb mumbling in his dreams.

But Telly remained still.

Alone.

Knees drawn to his chest, eyes locked on the dying embers. They pulsed red, then black, then red again— like a slow heartbeat echoing in the silence. His fingers tingled. Not from heat, but something deeper. Something pulling.

The feeling grew, spreading up his arms, through his chest, until it wrapped around his spine like a coil of static and breath.

And then it happened.

The vision.

Not like a dream. Not like the earlier pulses that came in flashes or hunches.

This was different.

This was a storm.

It hit like a wave crashing through a broken dam—rushing, roaring, too loud to fight. He closed his eyes and it opened wider.

He saw a boy—screaming behind glass, his fists pounding against a steel-reinforced window, mouth forming words no one could hear.

A girl strapped to a table, white-coated figures circling her. Electrodes wired to her temples. Her eyes glowed—not with power, but with fear.

A man—middle-aged, bruised, bleeding—chained to a chair in a dark room. His body pulsed with light so intense it cracked the walls around him. His eyes were open, but unfocused, as though part of him had already left.

And in the center of it all—scorched into the floor, burned into every surface—was the mark.

Two intersecting circles.

Now glowing.

Now burning.

Now watching.

Telly gasped, his body snapping backward.

He hit the floor, lungs seizing, the vision clawing at his brain even as it faded. The firelight flickered beside him, now no more than embers and ash.

His breath caught in his throat, raw and shallow.

Then a voice.

"You saw it."

Sera stood in the doorway, her silhouette framed by the cold blue edge of dawn. She wasn't surprised. Her eyes held no fear—only confirmation.

He nodded, wiping sweat from his neck with a trembling hand.

"They've found another," she said quietly. "And this one doesn't even know what they are yet."

Telly pulled himself up slowly, limbs shaking as the last echoes of the vision faded. The fire crackled behind him, as if something in it still remembered.

He looked at her, his voice dry.

"Where?"

Sera stepped forward and placed a folded slip of paper into his palm.

A name. A town. Coordinates scrawled in black ink.

"We leave at first light," she said.

Behind them, the fire whispered one last time and collapsed into coals.

James R. Baldwin

FORTY

The Next Name

The next morning, the group packed quickly and quietly. Sera, Ash, Caleb, Noor, and Telly left the chapel just after dawn, following Sera's slip of paper coordinates.

They traveled west by backroads and footpaths, avoiding cameras and populated towns. After nearly two days, they reached the edge of a small farming community tucked against low hills in Nebraska.

The name on the paper: Micah Lane. Fourteen. No known family. Foster system. Trouble sleeping. Trouble with storms.

"He's been bouncing between homes for years," Noor explained. "Labeled 'emotionally unstable.' Every time he has a meltdown, something breaks. Trees fall. Power lines fry. They think it's a coincidence. We don't."

They scoped out the foster home from a distance—an aging farmhouse with a barn and broken fencing.

"He doesn't know what he is," Caleb said. "But I'd bet anything he feels it."

Telly watched from the tree line as a boy emerged from the house. Skinny, dark-haired, hollow-eyed. He looked... haunted.

"He's already pulling storms," Ash muttered. "Look at the clouds."

Above, the sky churned, though the radar had called for clear skies.

Sera turned to Telly. "You're the one he'll listen to."

Telly nodded. "Then let's bring him home."

James R. Baldwin

FORTY-ONE

The Raid

They waited until nightfall. The farmhouse lights dimmed, and the wind carried the sharp tang of ozone—Micah's storms were stirring.

Telly moved first. He crossed the field slowly, hands raised, every step measured. The others remained in the treeline, watching.

Micah stood by the barn now, alone, watching the clouds churn.

"Micah," Telly said gently. "I'm like you."

Micah didn't answer. His eyes flicked toward the house, then back to the sky.

"I know what it's like," Telly continued. "When it starts to build inside. When you don't know what to do with it."

"I didn't mean to hurt anyone," Micah whispered.

"I believe you."

Telly took another step.

And that's when the van pulled up.

Black. Silent. No headlights.

Doors flung open. Figures in tactical gear surged toward them.

"Go!" Ash's voice cut through the wind as the team moved from cover.

Telly grabbed Micah's wrist. "Run with me."

The boy hesitated, but followed.

Sera deflected a tranquilizer dart with a swipe of her staff. Noor scattered gravel with her mind, blinding one of the agents. Caleb pulled two flash grenades from his coat and threw them hard into the dark.

The night lit up.

In the chaos, Telly and Micah reached the treeline.

But one dart struck Caleb in the leg.

He staggered.

Ash grabbed him and dragged him back as Sera laid cover.

By the time the vans regrouped, the group had vanished into the forest.

Micah, breathing hard, looked at Telly.

"Who are you people?"

Telly met his gaze.

"Awakened," he said. "Like you."

FORTY-TWO

Sacrifice

The forest was darker than usual that night—thick clouds blocked the moon, and the silence was too complete.

They didn't stop until they were miles from the farm, Micah moving with them now, stunned but alert.

Caleb limped more with each step, the tranquilizer slowing his body, fogging his mind.

"We need to stop," Noor said. "He's not going to make it at this pace."

Ash spun on her. "We stop now, we're a target. You want to help him? Then carry him."

Sera intervened, pressing her palm to Caleb's chest. "He needs rest, but we can buy time."

She pulled a vial from her satchel and gave him a few drops. His breathing evened slightly.

Still, he couldn't walk.

"We'll have to split," Ash said. "Two groups. One draws them away, one gets the healer out."

Telly hesitated. "I'm not leaving him."

"You're not," Ash said. "I am."

They argued quietly. But in the end, Ash took Caleb over his shoulder and vanished into the dark with Noor.

Telly, Sera, and Micah went the opposite way, doubling back along the creek line.

By morning, only three made it to the rendezvous point.

No sign of Ash.

No sign of Caleb.

Just a signal left behind—two intersecting circles scratched into a fallen log.

He was alive.

But the war had claimed its first cost.

And it wouldn't be the last."

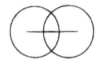

FORTY-THREE

Reckoning

The rendezvous point was a cave hidden behind a narrow waterfall deep in the canyon woods. It was cramped, cold, and silent—but for now, it was safe.

Telly sat near the water's edge with Micah and Sera, their backs to the stone, waiting.

Noor and Ash hadn't returned. Caleb hadn't sent another sign.

The tension gnawed.

"They won't make it back," Micah finally said. "Will they?"

Telly didn't answer. He couldn't—not yet.

Sera crouched by the fire, fingers flicking embers into the air. "They knew the risk. That's why they chose to go."

Telly looked up. "Then we honor them by not wasting it."

He pulled out the flash drive Ash had recovered.

"We stop running," he said. "We find the others. We expose what they're doing. And we take this to the world."

Sera raised an eyebrow. "You want to go public?"

Telly nodded. "Not now. Not loud. But controlled. Carefully. We build something bigger than a circle in chalk."

Micah shifted. "That makes you the leader, doesn't it?"

Telly paused.

"No," he said. "It makes us a movement."

He looked at the fire, its reflection in the dark water beside them.

"Because next time... we don't run. Next time—we fight."

The Touch of Telly D. Young

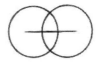

FORTY-FOUR

Ashes and Echoes

Two nights later, a radio signal broke the silence. Three short pulses. One long. Then a gap. Sera sat up first. "That's them."

Telly rushed to the pack where they'd hidden the receiver, tuning to the buried channel. More pulses followed—erratic, broken by static—but unmistakable.

Ash.

No voice, no code, but the rhythm was his. Caleb was still alive.

But it wasn't just a message.

It was a warning.

By sunrise, the cave was empty. The trio moved east through narrow canyons and thick brush, following the trail Ash had embedded in the signal: a series of pings pointing toward a silo just outside an abandoned military town.

It took them a day and a half.

What they found wasn't a trap, but close.

Caleb was there—barely conscious, bleeding from a gash on his side, hidden beneath tarp and brush. Noor knelt beside him, exhausted and bruised. She didn't speak until they'd helped her carry him to safety.

"They found us," she whispered. "But they didn't expect us to fight back."

Ash hadn't made it back with her.

Not yet.

That night, Telly sat beside Caleb's sleeping form. Noor lay nearby, recovering.

The fire was low.

Sera broke the silence. "You said this was a movement. Then let's make it one."

Telly nodded slowly.

He didn't feel ready. But maybe no one ever was.

"We find the rest," he said. "And then we burn down the places where they try to hide us."

FORTY-FIVE

Blueprints

The fire burned low, its glow dancing across the cavern's uneven stone walls they claimed as a temporary base. The low crackle of the flames mixed with the rhythmic dripping of water from the ceiling, like a slow, steady heartbeat echoing off the stone. A faint breeze wafted in through the cave's narrow mouth, carrying the earthy scent of wet pine and distant rain. The air inside was damp and smelled faintly of smoke and moss. Long roots hung from cracks in the ceiling like natural chandeliers, and shallow pools of cold water reflected flickering light across the stone floor.

A narrow opening on the far wall let in streaks of fading daylight, just enough to hint at a thick forest beyond. Outside, the wind stirred the trees with a whispering hiss, and somewhere in the distance, an owl called out—low and haunting. Their voices echoed faintly in the hollow space, reminding them that even in hiding, silence was fragile. its glow danced across the cavern walls they'd claimed as a temporary base. Noor sat cross-legged with a laptop on her knees, cables stretched to a portable power pack humming softly in the corner.

Sera passed a cup of water to Caleb, who leaned against the stone with a blanket over his shoulders. His breathing was steady, but every movement looked like it cost him.

Telly stood over the spread of maps and notes, the stolen flash drive blinking from a port in Noor's device.

"It's not just surveillance," Noor said. "It's infrastructure. Safehouse locations, redacted field agents, and this—Project Silencer. That's their playbook. And if this is real, they're already running trials."

Micah hovered near the entrance, listening more than speaking. He pointed at one of the screens. "What if we send something back? A message. Not just to them—to the others. The ones hiding."

Telly looked at him. "A broadcast?"

Micah nodded. "Coded. But clear. If I were still alone, I'd want to know someone was out there."

Caleb coughed. "We can't just light flares and hope no one notices. If we send a signal, they'll follow it."

"Then we make them follow it," Sera said. "And while they chase smoke, we build something solid."

Telly drew a circle on the map. Then three more. Each mark represented more than a place—it represented a promise. A place where one of them would stand watch, offer refuge, become a point of light in a darkening web.

"We'll need scouts," Noor said. "People who can move unseen and report back without drawing attention."

"Encryptions too," added Sera. "We need layers of code, fallback signals, and backup routes for anyone who might find us."

Micah, still near the entrance, finally stepped forward. "I'll help. I don't know all of this, but I can feel things—weather, pressure. I think I can sense people too. Emotions maybe. It's... not just storms anymore."

Caleb gave a tired smile. "We'll need all of that. Every piece."

"Beacons," he said. "Safe nodes. We don't just run anymore. We root. We build."

The others watched him, the silence stretching long and steady.

Telly held their gaze, his voice quiet but unwavering.

"This isn't just about making it through anymore. This is the start of something bigger."

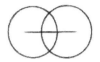

FORTY-SIX

The First Beacon

They moved before dawn.

The forest was still damp with the night's rainfall, the ground soft beneath their boots. Telly, Noor, and Micah traveled east toward an abandoned ranger station tucked deep in a stretch of old-growth forest. It had been marked on one of the stolen maps—an outpost once used for wildfire monitoring, long since forgotten.

"This is where we start," Telly said, pushing through a curtain of ferns. "If it's clear, we set up. If not, we move on."

The station came into view like a ghost—weather-worn wood, broken windows, vines creeping up its sides. But it still stood. Still shelter.

They entered cautiously. Noor swept each room. No recent activity.

"It'll take work," she said, "but it's defensible."

Micah stood in the center of the main room, eyes closed. "It feels... quiet. Not empty. Safe."

Telly knelt beside the fireplace, where a faded emblem of a ranger badge had been carved into the stone. He touched it briefly, then opened his pack.

Out came the first beacon: a small, solar-powered transmitter wrapped in canvas and copper shielding. Noor placed it in the attic, beneath a gap in the roof where sunlight streamed through.

"Encryption will take an hour," she said. "After that, it's live."

Telly exhaled slowly.

Their first light in the dark.

The message wouldn't be loud. It wouldn't name them. But for those listening, it would say enough:

You're not alone. Find the signal. Find us."

The Touch of Telly D. Young

James R. Baldwin

FORTY-SEVEN

Ripples

Three days later, the first answer came.

A flicker of response in the beacon's low-frequency band—just a single tone, followed by coordinates. Noor traced it to a warehouse outside Des Moines.

"Could be one of us," she said. "Could be a trap."

They voted. Telly, Sera, and Micah would go. Noor and Caleb would stay behind and reinforce the beacon in case someone else showed.

The trip took a day and a half, mainly moving by night.

The warehouse was dark. Silent. A rusted chain-link gate sagged at the front. Telly felt the pull before he even stepped inside.

She was waiting.

A girl. Maybe seventeen. Blonde hair chopped short. Burn scars up one arm. She didn't flinch when they entered.

"You sent the signal?" Telly asked.

She nodded. "Name's Rowan."

Sera stepped forward. "What's your gift?"

Rowan looked at the floor. "I can break things. Machines. Power. Electricity. I touch it, and it dies."

Micah blinked. "We could use that."

Telly took a step closer. "Do you want to come with us?"

Rowan hesitated. Then nodded. "If I stay here, they'll find me. If I go with you... maybe I finally get to fight back."

Outside, the wind stirred the leaves. The signal had found someone.

And the ripples were just beginning.

James R. Baldwin

FORTY-EIGHT

Rowan

Before she was Rowan, she was just a foster kid named Sarah Jo. She grew up bouncing between homes—never in one place long enough to unpack everything. The only constants were her quiet defiance and the strange malfunctions that always followed her.

The first time it happened, she was ten. Her foster father's truck wouldn't start for three days—right after he'd slammed a door near her face. Then it was the microwave shorting out. A phone catching fire in someone's hand. A laptop that died mid-sentence when a caseworker typed the word removal.

They said she was bad luck. A jinx.

But Rowan knew better.

By fourteen, she could feel it humming beneath her skin. Power lines made her teeth buzz. Engines coughed around her. If she got too close to live wires, the lights dimmed.

At fifteen, she ran.

She found work in scrap yards and shelters, always near machines, always careful not to touch too much. But word started to spread—about people like her. And about others going missing.

She burned her old ID. Changed her name to Rowan.

By the time the beacon's signal reached her, she was already watching the skies.

And when Telly and the others stepped into that warehouse, she didn't hesitate because she hadn't hoped for rescue.

She'd been preparing for war.

FORTY-NINE

Static

The return trip from the warehouse was tense. Rowan rode in silence, her eyes constantly scanning the treeline beyond the road. The truck's worn tires hummed against the gravel, a steady background to the crunch of shifting gear and the wind brushing low pine branches. Every time a bird took flight or the wind shifted direction, she flinched slightly—reflexes hardened by years of surviving alone.

The sun filtered through the trees in angled beams, catching in the dust and grit that clung to their clothes. They passed a rusted highway sign half-swallowed by kudzu, its letters too worn to read.

Micah, riding in the backseat, tried to break the quiet. "You ever try to control it? What you do to machines?"

Rowan gave a short shake of her head. "Not really. It's not like flipping a switch. It's more like... holding a live wire and trying not to fry the circuit."

"Sounds familiar," Telly murmured from behind the wheel, eyes fixed ahead.

They arrived at the beacon just before dusk. The forest wrapped around the station like a protective veil. Fog clung low to the forest floor, and the chirp of cicadas was beginning to rise in the growing stillness.

Noor was outside adjusting the signal shielding. She didn't flinch when Rowan approached—just studied her like a new equation. Her gaze was sharp, clinical, but not unkind.

"Welcome," she said. "We don't have time to waste."

Inside, Caleb was awake, sitting up against the wall with a map across his lap. Pale, but lucid.

"We got another ping," he said. "Weak. Out of Missouri."

"Could be interference," Noor added. "Or someone new."

Rowan's jaw tensed. "Or someone listening."

Telly looked around at the faces in the room—some worn, some wary, all watching him now. A small fire crackled in the hearth behind them, casting long shadows across the floor.

"We're not hiding from static anymore," he said. "We chase it. If someone's reaching back, we need to find them."

Rowan crossed her arms. "Then we better move fast. Noise draws hunters."

Caleb circled the coordinates on the map with a trembling finger. "Then let's make sure we're the ones who get there first."

The return trip from the warehouse was tense. Rowan rode in silence, her eyes constantly scanning the treeline beyond the road. Every time a bird took flight or the wind shifted, she flinched slightly—reflexes hardened by years of surviving alone.

Micah tried to break the quiet. "You ever try to control it? What you do to machines?"

Rowan gave a short shake of her head. "Not really. It's not like flipping a switch. It's more like... holding a live wire and trying not to fry the circuit."

"Sounds familiar," Telly murmured.

They arrived at the beacon just before dusk.

Noor was outside adjusting the signal shielding. She didn't flinch when Rowan approached—just studied her like a new equation.

"Welcome," she said. "We don't have time to waste."

Inside, Caleb was awake, sitting up against the wall with a map across his lap. "We got another ping. Weak. Out of Missouri."

"Could be interference," Noor added. "Or someone new."

Rowan's jaw tensed. "Or someone listening."

Telly looked around at the faces in the room—some worn, some wary, all watching him now.

"We're not hiding from static anymore," he said. "We chase it. If someone's reaching back, we need to find them."

Rowan crossed her arms. "Then we better move fast. Noise draws hunters."

Caleb circled the coordinates on the map. "Then let's make sure we're the ones who get there first."

FIFTY

Echoes in Missouri

The journey into Missouri took longer than expected.

Fog clung to the hills like draped cloth, and the roads narrowed the farther they drove. The ping from the beacon had been weak—fragmented data, no name, no voice. But it had a pulse. And in a world where silence was dangerous, pulses meant life.

They moved in a single vehicle—an old station wagon Micah had hotwired from a salvage yard two towns over. Telly drove. Rowan navigated from the passenger seat, maps splayed across her lap. Sera and Micah rode in the back, weapons and supplies tucked beneath the seats.

No one spoke much. Every turn of the road felt like a decision.

By nightfall, they reached the edge of the coordinates: an abandoned motel swallowed by overgrowth, just off a forgotten two-lane highway. The sign out front had lost its neon years ago, but the word "Rest" was still visible in peeling red paint.

Telly stepped out first.

The air smelled like damp wood and ozone. Somewhere nearby, thunder rumbled low—not loud, not close, but steady.

Micah closed his eyes. "It's not a storm," he whispered. "It's someone."

They approached the building slowly. One door was ajar.

Inside, the air was dry. Still.

Then—movement.

A figure stepped from the shadows. A boy. Maybe sixteen. Eyes wide. Hands raised.

"Please," he said. "I didn't mean to call anyone. I didn't even know I could."

Telly stepped forward, his voice calm. "It's okay. We're not here to hurt you."

The boy's name was Eli. And like them, he was waking up.

But unlike them—he wasn't alone.

From behind the motel, another signal flared.

And this one wasn't friendly."

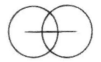

FIFTY-ONE

Shadows at the Door

The second flare came in a sharp burst of light—a flash that lit the treetops behind the motel and died just as quickly. Telly turned instinctively, shielding Eli with one arm as Rowan and Sera dropped into defensive stances.

"Micah," Telly said. "Where is it?"

Micah was already reaching out, palms down, eyes half-lidded. "East. Close. Moving slow."

Rowan reached into her coat and handed Telly a short-range jammer. "If they're tracking his pulse, this'll buy us two minutes."

Eli's breathing sped up. "Who are they?"

Sera knelt beside him. "Not friends. But you're not alone anymore. Do you understand?"

He nodded shakily.

They moved quickly—out the back of the motel and into the woods, sticking to the shadows.

From the edge of the trees, Telly caught a glimpse of the figures emerging from the dark: two, maybe three. Not soldiers. Something worse.

Black uniforms. No insignia. Visors that hummed faintly in the night.

"They're not here to talk," Rowan whispered.

Sera touched the small communicator on her wrist. "Noor. Incoming. Missouri site. Send backup and bury the beacon."

Static. Then Noor's voice: "Acknowledged. Moving."

Telly turned to Eli. "Can you run?"

"Yes."

"Then follow me. And don't stop until I say."

They disappeared into the trees just as the motel behind them erupted in a pulse of energy.

The chase had begun.

James R. Baldwin

FIFTY-TWO

Threshold

They ran until their lungs burned.

The Missouri woods were thick with fog, turning every tree into a silhouette and every shadow into a question. The motel had vanished behind them, swallowed by night and the pulse of whatever tech weapon had been deployed. Still, they didn't stop. Not until they reached the creek.

Telly signaled a halt with a raised hand. They crouched low beneath the thickets, breathing hard, the sound of boots and brush cracking faintly behind them.

"They're sweeping in a pattern," Sera whispered, watching the glint of movement through the trees. "Grid search. Military-style, but faster."

Micah gritted his teeth, closing his eyes. "They're using something else—some kind of pressure sweep. I can feel it rippling."

Rowan stepped forward. "Then I kill the tech."

"No," Telly said firmly. "We don't strike unless we have no choice. We still don't know what they're capable of."

Eli was shaking. "I'm sorry. I didn't know anyone could hear me. I didn't mean to pull anyone in."

"You didn't," Telly said, gripping his shoulder. "You reached out. That's what matters."

A hum filled the air. Low, vibrating. Then a faint blue glow shimmered between the trees ahead.

"They're using a perimeter drone," Sera said. "It's mapping signatures."

Rowan took a step toward it. "I can disable it. No explosion, no heat spike. Just silence."

Telly hesitated, then nodded.

Rowan vanished into the brush.

Seconds stretched like hours. Then—darkness. The hum ceased.

Sera exhaled. "We've got a gap. But not for long."

Telly looked at the others. "We cross the creek. After that, we don't stop until we're clear of this grid."

Eli wiped his face with a trembling sleeve. "What's after the creek?"

Telly didn't smile.

"The next threshold. And the rest of your life."

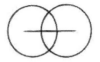

FIFTY-THREE

Crossing Lines

The creek was fast and biting cold, swollen with snowmelt from the mountains. Telly went first, water pushing past his knees as the stones shifted underfoot. The current pulled hard—a reminder of how even solid ground could give way without warning.

Eli followed close behind, teeth chattering, his small hand clamped around Micah's. Sera moved last, her eyes scanning the opposite bank for movement, and every step was measured and alert.

When they reached the far side, they dropped low into the brush, soaking wet and breathing hard.

"Signal?" Telly asked, glancing toward Rowan, who was crouched over a slim sensor clipped to her belt.

She shook her head. "We bought distance, but not silence. They're still tracking."

Caleb's voice crackled faintly over the comms. "We're redirecting the Missouri beacon to broadcast misdirection pulses. It should buy you twelve, maybe fifteen minutes if they're using automated tracking."

"Copy," Sera said. "We'll make it count."

They moved fast, keeping low through the thickets and ravines, moving between deer trails and dry gullies. Telly knew they were close to pushing Eli too hard, but stopping now meant capture.

At a ridge above the river, they paused.

Rowan turned to Telly. "You know we're crossing a line, right? The next time we do this, it might not be a clean escape. It might be fire."

Telly nodded slowly. "I know."

She held his gaze. "And you're still sure?"

He looked back down the trail. "I was sure the first time I touched someone and they stood back up."

Below, the woods began to echo with the first distant thud of boots on the wrong path.

For now.

They had crossed the water. But the line they'd just stepped over?

It was war.

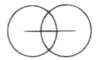

FIFTY-FOUR

The Trap

The signal came mid-morning.

A faint ping, just outside of their range, marked in the same digital cadence as the beacon network. Noor caught it first from the chapel bunker.

"Another response?" Caleb asked, hunched over the receiver.

Noor narrowed her eyes. "Maybe. It's repeating too cleanly. Like it wants to be found."

Rowan's voice crackled over the comms. "Could be bait."

"Or a cry for help," Telly replied. "Either way, we check it out. We don't leave signals unanswered."

They split into two teams.

Telly, Sera, and Rowan followed the signal to a crumbling industrial site west of the last ping. Rusted scaffolding rose like skeletal towers over cracked asphalt and shattered windows. Pigeons burst from the eaves as they stepped inside.

Micah and Eli stayed behind with Caleb, monitoring the perimeter from a secured position in the foothills.

Sera scanned the space. "Feels wrong. Like it's been swept."

Rowan knelt beside a rusted terminal box, fingers ghosting the wires. "Too clean. This place is dead but... dressed up to look alive."

Telly moved toward the center of the open floor—what once had been a loading dock. His breath caught.

A single item waited in the light.

A photo.

Of his parents.

Pinned to a chair with a steel spike through the center.

Behind him, the floor clicked.

"Move!" Rowan shouted.

Too late.

The room erupted in sound—steel shutters slamming closed, sirens blaring, floodlights flaring to life.

Telly turned to run.

But the trap had already closed.

James R. Baldwin

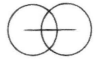

FIFTY-FIVE

Confrontation

Floodlights flared from every angle, burning through the dust and casting long shadows across the cracked floor. Above, mechanical shutters sealed the windows with a violent grind of rusted steel.

Telly ducked behind a rusted cart as shouts echoed through the building. Boots thundered on metal walkways above.

Rowan was already moving. She slipped behind a power conduit and reached for the control panel. Sparks danced beneath her fingertips.

Sera flanked right, her blade already drawn, eyes locked on the first shape breaching the threshold.

Black visor. Silent. Weapon raised.

Telly stepped out with his hands lifted. "You don't want this. You don't even know what you're fighting."

The figure didn't answer—only opened fire.

A bolt of nonlethal current cracked the air, striking the wall where Telly had stood a second earlier.

Rowan snarled and slapped her palm against the conduit. The lights flickered. The air went still.

And then—the power died.

The silence was deafening.

Sera moved first. She struck low, fast, disarming the lead agent in a blink. Telly followed, tackling another before he could recover.

They didn't kill. But they didn't hold back.

Outside, more vehicles approached.

"We have to go!" Rowan shouted. "Backup's coming in hot."

Telly dragged the chair with his parents' photo down into the shadows, snapping the picture free. His hand lingered on it just a second too long.

Sera grabbed his wrist. "Telly, now!"

They ran.

Out the back. Through a shattered loading door. Into the night.

The trap had closed.

But they'd broken it wide open.

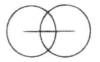

FIFTY-SIX

Fallout

The road out of the industrial zone wound through thickets of pine and abandoned railroad tracks, lit only by moonlight and the flicker of fire still licking at the trap they'd escaped.

They didn't stop running until the silence behind them felt real.

When they finally slowed, Telly bent over in the gravel, gasping. The photo of his parents was still crumpled in his hand, sweat smearing its edges.

Sera was the first to speak. "That was a message."

Rowan nodded. "Yeah. And they knew exactly what they were doing. That wasn't a kill order. That was psychological warfare."

Telly stared down the empty path ahead. "They're trying to fracture us. Break us before we get big enough to fight back."

Micah's voice crackled over the comms. "Are you safe?"

"For now," Sera replied. "But they saw us. Not just our shadows. Our faces."

Caleb came on next. "Then we're past subtle. We need to shift strategy. Go full signal lockdown and relocate all nodes west of the Mississippi."

Noor added, "And we build redundancy. Every time they try to scare us into hiding, we add two more places where we can stand."

Telly finally looked up, voice steady. "We build faster. Smarter. Louder if we have to. And next time… we're the ones setting the trap.

FIFTY-SEVEN

The Scars We Carry

They made it back to the beacon just before sunrise. The old ranger station glowed faintly from within, its windows covered with blackout curtains, the air inside thick with tension and exhaustion.

Caleb was waiting in the entryway, pale but upright, leaning on a cane fashioned from salvaged steel pipe.

"You made it," he said.

Telly gave a tight nod and handed him the photo, still folded. "They made it personal."

Caleb opened the picture slowly. His jaw tensed. "They've been holding this back. Waiting to use it until they thought it would break you."

"It didn't," Telly said. "But it left a mark."

Rowan walked straight to the basement server bank and began scanning logs for infiltration attempts. "We need a new firewall. They're inside our cycles—barely, but they're learning."

Sera slumped into a chair, exhaling. "We were almost baited into a kill box. If not for Rowan, we wouldn't be talking right now."

Noor entered quietly, a hot mug in her hands. She placed it in front of Telly. "You need to sleep."

Telly shook his head. "Not yet."

Micah, sitting against the wall, finally spoke. "Then maybe just sit. You don't have to carry it all at once."

Telly looked around the room. At the faces—tired, bruised, determined. Every one of them still standing.

He sat.

And for the first time in days, he let silence settle around him—not as an enemy, but a companion.

They were still whole.

Still here.

But the scars were settling in."

The Touch of Telly D. Young

James R. Baldwin

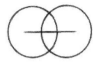

FIFTY-EIGHT

No More Ghosts

Later that day, the rain came.

It started as a whisper on the canopy above, then thickened into a steady drumbeat against the tin roof of the beacon. The scent of wet pine and earth drifted through the narrow windows as the group huddled around the main table.

Telly stood with a printed scan of the enemy photo in one hand. The original was sealed in a fireproof pouch, tucked into a lockbox beneath the station's floor.

"We need to talk about what this really is," he said.

Noor leaned forward, folding her hands. "We've crossed from shadows into spotlight. They know we're organizing. And they're targeting your past to shatter your future."

Sera nodded. "But it's not just you anymore. Every one of us has ghosts. They're trying to raise them."

Micah looked at the wall where Rowan had sketched out a new beacon design. "So we give our ghosts names. We bring them into the light."

Telly tapped the photo. "They think fear is a leash. Let's make it a compass."

Caleb's voice came low. "Then we bury the past with the future in mind. And we do it loudly."

Outside, thunder rolled.

Inside, the resolve hardened like steel in fire.

James R. Baldwin

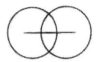

FIFTY-NINE

The Signal Breaks

The warning came just before midnight.

A burst of static across all frequencies. Not the usual interference—this was deeper. Violent. Like a scream trying to reach through silence. Then... nothing.

Noor sat up straight in her chair, headset still pressed to her ear. "We lost Denver."

Telly leaned over her shoulder. "Beacon?"

"Gone. Not just dark—gone. Like it never existed."

Rowan paced nearby. "Could it be sabotage? Or a sweep?"

Caleb pulled a paper map from the wall and pinned it flat. "That was one of our most remote nodes. No roads, no nearby towns. If they found it, they're inside the net."

Sera's voice was tight. "That wasn't random. They wanted us to hear it die."

Telly turned toward the center of the room. The group had gathered now—awake, alert, afraid but not frozen.

"They're not hunting signals anymore," he said. "They're erasing them."

Micah swallowed. "Like we were never there."

Telly looked at Rowan. "Can we build something they'll follow?"

Rowan raised an eyebrow. "A fake?"

"A trap."

Her expression shifted. "I can cook something dirty. Sloppy enough to bait them in, clean enough to convince them we're just stupid."

"Do it," Telly said. "And we'll be waiting when they come."

James R. Baldwin

SIXTY

Ash Returns

They didn't hear him at first.

It wasn't until Rowan stepped outside to test the signal bait that she caught a flicker of movement in the treeline. A limp. A figure wrapped in a worn coat, face shadowed beneath the hood.

She reached for her sidearm.

Then she heard the voice.

"Took you long enough to bait a trap worth walking into."

Rowan froze.

"Ash?"

He emerged slowly, one eye swollen shut, a deep cut bandaged with a strip of torn cloth. His posture was still solid, but something in his walk was off—pain tucked into every step.

"Easy," he said, raising a hand. "No one followed. I made sure."

Rowan led him inside without a word.

When Telly saw him, he didn't speak. Just crossed the room and gripped Ash's forearm, steady and fierce.

"You're alive."

"Barely," Ash rasped. "But alive enough to bring this."

From beneath his coat, he pulled a sealed drive and tossed it on the table. "It's not everything. But it's the final phase layout for Project Silencer. Names. Sites. Timelines."

Caleb took it like it was an artifact.

Noor leaned forward. "You stole this?"

Ash nodded. "And I paid for it. But they're shifting strategy. They're not just hunting you. They're preparing to replace you."

The room fell silent.

Telly closed his eyes. "Then it's time we do more than survive."

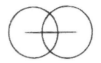

SIXTY-ONE

The Uprising

The message went out at dawn.

A short, encrypted burst on a dozen frequencies. No names. No demands. Just a voice—Telly's—calm and clear:

"You are not alone. If you can hear this, come. Bring nothing but yourself. You are enough."

It repeated twice. Then silence.

By dusk, they had confirmation.

Ping after ping lit up the map: Montana, Ohio, El Paso, a refugee camp outside St. Louis. Micah watched the dots appear with growing awe.

"They heard us," he whispered.

And they came.

***

The foothills above the beacon transformed into something new: a convergence. Campfires. Portable shelters. Whispers of names and powers once spoken only in secret.

A boy who could see through walls. A woman who could wake memories in others. A mute girl whose shadows moved without her.

They arrived not for war—but for hope.

And then came the drone.

It buzzed in low from the north, silent until too close. Noor shouted a warning. Rowan fired a burst jammer. The drone dropped.

But it was already too late.

They were found.

And this time, they didn't run.

Ash stepped to the front line, rifle slung low. Sera stood beside him, blade drawn.

Telly moved to the center.

"If they want to erase us," he said, raising his voice for all to hear, "then let them see what they tried to wipe away."

He raised his hands.

And for the first time in public, he healed.

A fractured wrist. A burnt palm. A scarred eye.

And in that moment—under the trees, beside the fire—the world began to turn."

James R. Baldwin

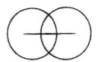

SIXTY-TWO

Revelation

The footage spread faster than they expected.

At first, it appeared only on encrypted channels. Then it leaked to private forums. A few hours later, a silent clip aired on a global news network—grainy, shaky, undeniable: a young man with blond hair laying his hands on the wounded, and the wounds fading.

They tried to scrub it. Too late.

By morning, the world knew.

Telly sat beneath the same tree where he had healed that night, the bark still scorched from where energy had surged. Around him, reporters had gathered like moths to flame—but they were kept back. The Awakened had formed a ring.

Noor stood beside him, a tablet in her hand, reading updates in real time. "Klemens has gone dark. Government lines are denying involvement. Some say they're launching an internal investigation. Others are calling it a hoax."

Telly looked up. "And the rest?"

She hesitated. "Some want to meet you. Others want to control you."

Ash, leaning against a tree, added, "And a few want to end you. But you knew that."

Telly nodded. "Yeah. I did."

Caleb limped forward, carrying the drive Ash had returned with. "There's more here than weapons and tactics," he said. "There are names. Research. The start of this—how it all began."

He opened the file.

Inside were scanned documents, decades old.

Project Silencer wasn't just a response.

It was the origin.

And somehow, it started with Telly's parents.

James R. Baldwin

SIXTY-THREE

The Light We Carry

The next morning dawned cold and cloudless. Mist hung low over the foothills, catching light as it rolled like smoke across the ground. The camp was quiet—too quiet—but not from fear. From awe.

Word had spread. Not just about Telly. About all of them. The world had seen something it couldn't explain. And for once, it didn't run.

Families showed up at the edge of the treeline. Journalists with hand-scrawled signs asking for peace. Doctors. Veterans. Survivors.

Noor counted thirty-seven new arrivals before breakfast. By noon, it was sixty.

Telly moved among them—not as a spectacle, but as a guide. He offered his hands when needed, his voice when asked, and his silence when that, too, was enough.

Micah helped organize meals. Sera taught basic defense to the new Awakened. Caleb translated raw data from the Project Silencer files into action plans and names to be protected.

But it wasn't until Rowan stood on the overlook above the valley and said, "They can't kill a fire that's everywhere," that Telly understood what they had become.

Not rebels. Not fugitives.

A movement.

That night, under stars too bright to ignore, Telly sat by the main fire and finally allowed himself a small smile.

They weren't hiding anymore.

They were carrying light.

And it was catching.

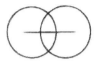

SIXTY-FOUR

Last Move

The peace didn't last.

Three nights after the world saw Telly heal, a signal lit up the private channels used by the original beacon founders. It wasn't from the Awakened.

It was from Klemens.

Encrypted. Short. One line:

"We warned you. Now we clean the board."

Noor dropped the tablet.

Rowan was already scanning air traffic logs. "They're mobilizing. Multiple convoys. Three blackbirds in the air. They're not chasing us anymore. They're sweeping."

Caleb unfolded the latest version of the beacon network map. "They're headed for the eastern chain first. We've got maybe twelve hours before they hit the Kentucky node. Then it's a domino fall."

Telly stared at the board. At the lights. At the lives.

Sera stepped forward. "We need to scatter. Evacuate the nodes. Take the data and burn the rest."

Ash shook his head. "We don't run from the last strike. We answer it."

Everyone looked to Telly.

He turned to Noor. "Can we hijack one of their signals?"

"With help," she said. "I'll need a rooftop. And time."

Telly nodded. "You'll have both."

He looked at Rowan. "Pick the loudest frequency."

Then, to the group:

"This is our last move. They wanted silence. We give them a signal so loud the whole world has to choose."

The Touch of Telly D. Young

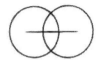

SIXTY-FIVE

Awakened

One year later.

The world had not ended. But it had changed.

The beacons were no longer hidden. What began as whispers of resistance had grown into a web of sanctuaries—places where the Awakened trained, taught, and healed in plain sight.

Project Silencer had collapsed under global scrutiny. Klemens had disappeared—some said trial, others exile, some whispered worse. No one cried for him.

And Telly?

He returned to where it began.

The old ranger station had become more than a safehouse. It was now a school, a sanctuary, and a monument. The walls had been repaired, the fires replaced with solar heat, the scars honored rather than hidden.

Telly stood outside under a wide blue sky, watching a new generation of Awakened spar in the clearing. A girl levitated pebbles while a boy reset a broken wrist with a flick of his fingers and a word of comfort.

Rowan leaned against the doorframe, arms crossed. "You still don't like speeches, huh?"

Telly smiled. "They don't need speeches. They need space. And each other."

Noor passed him a folded note. "More are coming. Always more."

He opened it. Coordinates. A new name.

Telly looked back once more at the clearing. At the light. At the faces.

"They're ready," he said.

Then he turned toward the trail, the wind at his back.

And walked into whatever came next.

James R. Baldwin

Book Two

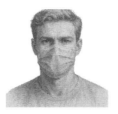

ONE

Beneath the Mask

Spring 2020

The world had locked its doors. Empty streets echoed with silence, and fear lingered like smoke in the air. COVID-19 had paralyzed cities, families, hope.

Telly sat on the rooftop of a shuttered clinic in Kansas City, watching a line of masked strangers wind around the block. He wore no symbol, no title, just a hoodie, jeans, and gloves. But even now, people whispered.

Whispered about the man who healed.

They didn't know his name. Only that he had appeared in parking lots, in alleyways, and once in a hospital's back hallway where the power had gone out and four patients on ventilators had begun to fail.

He had touched their hands.

And they had lived.

Now, they waited. Mothers with children. The elderly. A nurse on her third shift without sleep. No cameras. No claims. Just need.

Telly moved slowly down the fire escape, heart heavy with the weight of choice. He couldn't save them all. He knew that.

But maybe, today, he could save one.

And maybe, one was enough.

He stepped into the alley's light.

And the line straightened, as if hope had walked out of hiding.

Thank You

Dear Reader,

Thank you for joining us on this journey through *The Telly D. Young Series*. Your time, heart, and imagination are deeply appreciated. This story was born from a place of faith, loss, wonder, and the hope that light can rise even in the darkest corners of the world.

Every page written, every moment revealed, was for readers like you—who believe in purpose, redemption, and the power of what could be.

If this book moved you, inspired you, or gave you something to think about... we humbly ask:

Leave a Review

Your honest review helps more than you know. It guides other readers, supports independent publishing, and allows this series to continue growing.

Please take a moment to leave a rating or a short review on Amazon. Just a few words can go a long way.

Search "Telly D. Young" on Amazon or
Scan the QR code below to leave your review directly

From all of us at **Baldwin Book Publishing**, thank you.
We are honored to tell these stories—
And we're grateful to share them with you.

With all our heart,
The Baldwin Family

Made in the USA
Columbia, SC
30 June 2025